TONY BRADMAN

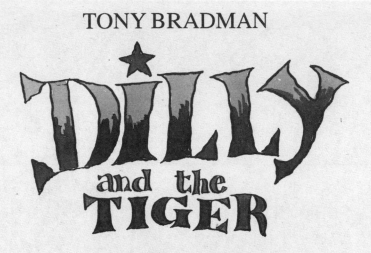

DILLY
and the
TIGER

and other stories

Cover and illustrations by Susan Hellard

DEAN

Dilly Goes Swamp Wallowing first published in Great Britain 1988
as *Dilly the Worst Day Ever*
Dilly and the Tiger first published in Great Britain 1988
Dilly and the Ghost first published in Great Britain 1989
Dilly Dinosaur, Superstar first published in Great Britain 1989
All by Piccadilly Press Limited

This omnibus edition published 1994 by Dean
an imprint of Reed Consumer Books Limited
Michelin House, 81 Fulham Road, London SW3 6RB
and Auckland, Melbourne, Singapore and Toronto

ISBN 0 603 55413 X

A CIP catalogue record for this title is available from the British Library

Printed in Great Britain by The Bath Press

CONTENTS

DILLY GOES SWAMP WALLOWING

DILLY AND THE TIGER

DILLY AND THE GHOST

DILLY DINOSAUR, SUPERSTAR

DILLY GOES SWAMP WALLOWING

I. DILLY AT THE LIBRARY

Did I ever tell you about the time Dilly was naughty at the library? I'll never forget it, and I don't think the dinosaurs who work there will either.

I love going to the library, because I love books. I can read really well, now – at school I'm on Level 8 Readers. At home I like reading the books about *The Famous Five Dinosaurs*. They're great.

Dilly loves books too, but he can't read yet, so Mother and Father still have to read to him. He likes picture books and stories about big bad creatures who chase little dinosaurs and try to gobble them up.

Sometimes we go to a bookshop to *buy* books. And sometimes we go to the library to *borrow* books. The only problem is that Dilly doesn't understand the difference.

"Come on, Dilly," said Father one day. "Get your books together. We've got to take them back today so you can get some new ones."

"But I don't want any new ones, Father," said Dilly. "I want to keep the books we bought at the library last week. They're mine."

"No, no, Dilly," Father laughed. "You don't *buy* books at the library. You only *borrow* them. You have to take them back once you've read them, so other people can read them too."

I could see that Dilly was looking
rather confused.

"So do we have to take back the
books we get from the bookshop, too?"
he said.

"No, Dilly," said Father. "You *buy*
books at the bookshop, so you can keep
them forever. Do you understand now,
Dilly?"

"Yes, Father," said Dilly. "I
understand."

But I don't think he did. He still
looked very confused, and at the library,
he did what he usually does – he

borrowed the same books he'd had before. Father tried to get him to have some new ones, but Dilly didn't want to.

"Are you sure you want the same books, Dilly?" Father said.

"Yes, Father," said Dilly. "They're my books, and I'm taking them home with me."

A week or so later, it was time to take our library books back. Father didn't even try to explain to Dilly about the difference between borrowing and buying. He just got the library books together and told Dilly that we were going.

"What's that you've got there, Dilly?" said Father just as we were leaving. Dilly was clutching a book under his arm.

"It's *The Three Little Dinosaurs*, Father," he said. Father sighed.

"That's not a library book, Dilly," he

said. "We *bought* that book at the Shopping Cave yesterday."

"I know, Father," said Dilly. "I just want to take it with me."

It took Father a while, but in the end he managed to persuade Dilly to leave *The Three Little Dinosaurs* at home.

Dilly was very well behaved at the library. He told Father that he would quite like to have some new books, this time, some books that he'd never read before. So he sat at a small table in the children's library looking through lots of different books while I chose mine. Father asked me to keep an eye on Dilly while he went into the grown-ups' library to choose his books, and get some for Mother, too. I said I would.

After a while, Father came back and said that it was time to go. I had the books I wanted, and Dilly had chosen his. We went to the counter where the librarian stamped everyone's books.

The library was crowded that day, so there was quite a queue. We were waiting behind another family, a Mother, Father and one small dinosaur who looked about the same age as Dilly. She was holding a book against her chest. She smiled at me, and then at Dilly.

But Dilly didn't smile back. I could
see that he had a very strange look on
his face, too. He looked rather cross.
The little dinosaur stopped smiling, and
backed towards her parents.

"Where did you get that book?" said
Dilly. "It's mine!"

"No it isn't," said the little dinosaur.
"It's mine!"

"Give it to me," said Dilly. He
reached towards her and tried to grab
the book.

"You can't have it!" said the little
dinosaur. "I won't let you!"

"Hey," said Father. "What's all this about? Don't be naughty, now, Dilly. It isn't your book. You've chosen yours, so leave the little dinosaur alone." He smiled at the little dinosaur's parents. Everyone in the queue was starting to look at us.

"But it is, Father," said Dilly. "It is my book!" Father looked quite cross now.

"I don't know how many times I've told you, Dilly," he said, "but you must try to understand. You can't keep the books you borrow from the library. Even if you've had that book before, it doesn't belong to you."

Dilly looked at Father . . . at the little dinosaur . . . and at everyone around him. I knew what was going to happen, and you do too, probably. He opened his mouth and . . . he let rip with an

ultra-special, 150-mile-per-hour super-
scream, the sort that makes librarians
duck under counters, grown-ups hide
behind the shelves, and little dinosaurs
bump into a big stack of books that fall
over. A grown-up tripped over the
books on the floor, and fell against some
more shelves . . . and they were
knocked over, too. By the time Dilly
had finished screaming, the library was
in an awful mess.

Father was very cross, and gave Dilly quite a telling off. I saw the little dinosaur looking at Dilly, and then I noticed what book she was holding.

It was *The Three Little Dinosaurs*.

Dilly thought she had his favourite book, the one he'd left at home! I told Father, and he explained to Dilly that it wasn't *his* book, it was the one that belonged in the library. It was exactly the same, but his one was safe at home. Father explained that there were thousands of copies of the same book in shops and libraries everywhere. Dilly didn't look as if he believed him.

But he did say sorry to the little dinosaur, and to the librarians, and he did help to tidy up the books that had been knocked over.

When we got home, he was sent straight up to his room as a punishment.

Later, though, at bedtime, I heard him talking to Father.

"Father," he said, "you know those other copies of *The Three Little Dinosaurs*, the ones you said were the

same as mine?"

"Yes, Dilly," said Father. "What about them?"

"Well," said Dilly, "I bet they're not as good as *my* one, are they?"

Father was quiet for a second.

"Dilly . . ." he started to say. Then I heard him sigh. "You're probably right, Dilly," he laughed. "I should think yours is the best one there is!"

II.   DILLY THE WORST DAY EVER

Dilly has always been naughty, but recently he's been a lot worse. It seems that Mother and Father have to tell him off and send him to his room at least two or three times a day.

Yesterday, for instance, Dilly started misbehaving as soon as he got out of bed. Mother told him to go into the bathroom to have a wash and have his teeth cleaned, but he wouldn't. He just stamped his foot and made a horrible face.

"I won't, I won't, I won't," he said. "I hate toothpaste. It's smelly and yucky!"

I thought for a moment that Mother was going to lose her temper. But she didn't. Instead, she just sighed.

"Dilly," she said, "I think you must be the naughtiest, most stubborn little dinosaur in the whole, wide world."

"I am NOT!" shouted Dilly, and stamped his foot again.

"Oh yes you are," said Mother. "Why, I don't think you could be good for a whole day if you tried."

"I could, I could!" shouted Dilly.

"All right, Dilly," said Mother. "If you think you can, why don't you prove it? Why don't you try and be good for the rest of today? And if you are good, perhaps we'll give you a little treat."

Dilly didn't shout this time. He smiled.

"What kind of treat, Mother?" he said in his softest, best behaved voice.

"Oh, I don't know, Dilly . . . " she said. "Something nice, I should think. You'll just have to wait and see. Well? Are you going to be good today?"

Dilly smiled again.

"Yes, Mother," he said. "I will." And then he marched into the bathroom, and stood by the basin, waiting to have his

teeth cleaned and to be washed.

At breakfast, Dilly ate all his fern flakes and toasted fern stalks without making any mess at all. He didn't put his elbows on the table, or knock over his pineapple juice, like he usually does. And afterwards, he helped Father to tidy everything away.

"Well, Dilly," said Father. "You are being very helpful today."

Dilly just smiled, and asked Father to pass him the next thing to put away. It was his favourite cup, the one with his name on, the one he always drank his pineapple juice from.

But as Father handed it to him, it fell

to the floor – and smashed into tiny pieces. Dilly looked upset.

"Oh, Dilly," said Father. "You must be more careful . . . still, never mind. I'll finish up here. You run along and play."

Dilly did run along and play, which was surprising. Usually he pesters Mother or Father to play with him, or let him watch cartoons on TV. But today he said he was going to play houses, and went into the garden.

Dilly isn't very patient, but he spent ages making a house. First he put a blanket down on the ground by the giant fern, and then he hung another from a branch to make a roof. He laid out all his toys, and he even said that I could play with him if I wanted to.

"My, my, Dilly," said Mother. "That looks like an interesting game. You see

how much fun it can be if you spend less
time being naughty and more time
playing?"

Dilly smiled. He looked really pleased
with himself.

But just at that moment, a big, black
cloud passed over the sun. The sky went
very dark, and it turned quite chilly.
Then some little drops of rain began to
fall. They pitter-pattered on the fern
leaves and on Dilly's house. Mother said

she thought there was going to be a storm.

She was right. Soon the little drops of rain had become great fat drops that poured from the sky. We had to rush to take Dilly's house apart and get everything in before it all got soaked.

Dilly looked fed up.

"Never mind, Dilly," said Mother. "It might be sunny again later. Then you can go outside to play again."

But it didn't get sunny later. It rained, and rained, and rained. We had to stay indoors all day.

Now usually on days like that, Dilly gets bored. And when Dilly gets bored, he gets really naughty and does all the things he shouldn't. Today was different, though. He played in his room for a while, and then he came downstairs and asked Mother if there was anything he could do to help her. She looked really surprised.

"Oh . . . er . . . well, Dilly," she said, "there's nothing you can do for me at the moment. How about tidying your room?"

"I've already done that," he said with a smile.

"You have?" said Mother. "Well, as you're being so good today, perhaps you'd like to watch some TV. I think there are some cartoons on today."

"Is it *Stan the Stegosaurus?*" asked Dilly. It's one of his favourites.

"Yes, I think it is," said Mother. "I don't know why you like it so much,

Dilly . . . It's not on for a while, so you'll have to be patient."

Dilly *was* patient. He didn't pester Mother to turn on the TV, although I could see that he was getting very excited. The time for the programme came round at last. Mother switched on the TV . . . but nothing happened. There was no sound, and no picture. Mother turned it off and on again, but still nothing happened.

The TV set was broken.

Mother phoned the repair dinosaur, but he couldn't come until the next day.

So we wouldn't be able to watch TV at all.

Dilly looked so disappointed when Mother told him the bad news.

"Never mind, Dilly," said Mother. "But I tell you what . . . why don't I phone Dixie's mother and ask if Dixie can come over to play with you this afternoon?"

Dilly started smiling again. Dixie's his best friend, and he just loves to play with her.

"Oh, yes please, Mother," he said.

"OK, Dilly," said Mother. "You can be thinking of what games to play while I'm on the phone."

Mother phoned . . . but it turned out

that Dixie had a cold, and couldn't come
out.

Now Dilly looked even more
disappointed than ever.

"Never . . . " Mother started to say.

"I know, Mother," said Dilly. "Never
mind." He went off to his room looking
very fed up.

Things went from bad to worse for
poor Dilly. He was still trying hard to be
good, but nothing seemed to go right for
him. A wheel came off one of his
favourite toy dino-cars while he was
playing with it. Then he tripped over a
rug and bumped his snout. And finally,

when he was coming out of the kitchen,
I shut his tail in the door. It looked as if

it hurt quite a lot.

Normally, Dilly would have shouted and screamed and maybe even hit me. But he didn't complain at all, although I could see that he really wanted to. It was getting harder and harder for him to

keep his temper, although Mother and Father didn't notice it – they were too busy. In fact, when Dilly tripped over the rug, Father said he hoped he wasn't going to start running around and being naughty. And when he got his tail caught in the door, Mother said he ought to look where he was going.

Later, Dilly asked if he could have a drink, and Mother gave him some pineapple juice. She put it on the table, and went out of the room. I had a drink too, and when I picked mine up, I knocked Dilly's over. There was pineapple juice all over the table, and it was dripping on to the carpet.

Then Mother came back into the room.

"Dilly Dinosaur," she said, "why do you always knock your drink over? And I thought you said you were going to be good all day today!"

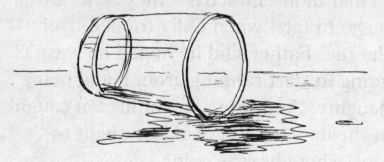

"But Mother . . . " said Dilly.

"Don't you give me any of your 'buts', Dilly," she said. "Look at the mess!"

"But Mother . . . " I started to say.

"And you stay out of it, too, Dorla," she said. "Dilly, go and get a cloth immediately!"

I looked at Dilly, and he looked at me. I was going to try and tell Mother the truth, but it was too late. Before I could open my mouth, Dilly opened his . . . and fired off an ultra-special, 150-mile-per-hour super-scream. When he was quiet, Mother told him off and sent him to his room.

I managed to tell Mother the truth in the end. She went up to see Dilly while I was clearing up the spilt pineapple juice.

Dilly was very upset, she told me later. He said he had tried so hard to be good, and not to scream, but everything had gone wrong and he just couldn't keep it in any more. And now he wasn't going to get his treat.

But Mother said it wasn't his fault,
and he had been very, very, very good
all day. So he could have his treat after
all. In fact we could *all* have a treat.
Mother and Father were going to take us
swamp wallowing the very next day.
Dilly and I were so pleased.

And do you know what Dilly said
when he went to bed?

"Mother," he said, "that was my
worst day ever. Is it OK if I don't try so
hard to be good tomorrow?"

"I should think so, Dilly," she
laughed. "I don't know whether I could
get used to you being good all the time,
anyway!"

III. DILLY GOES SWAMP
WALLOWING

Mother and Father say that every young
dinosaur should learn to swamp wallow
properly. The Swamp can be a
dangerous place, and you need to learn
how to stay afloat, and what to do when
the mud's too sticky.

That's why I have swamp wallowing
lessons. I love them, too. In fact, they're
my favourite thing. I've got badges for
swamp wallowing as well – Father sewed
them on my costume.

So I was pleased when Mother said we could go to The Swamp as a treat. When we got there, the mud was lovely and warm, and Mother took me down the slide. Father wallowed with Dilly in the shallow end, and we all had a great time.

Dilly enjoyed himself so much he said he didn't want to get out when it was time to go home.

"But I'm afraid you've got to, Dilly," said Mother. "Come along, now. Don't be naughty."

Dilly didn't say anything. But I could see that he was thinking of being very naughty indeed. He opened his mouth the way he does when he's about to let loose a 150-mile-per-hour super-scream . . . then Mother said something that stopped him.

"Come on, Dilly. Let's go and ask in the office if you can start having some swamp wallowing lessons."

Dilly closed his mouth without screaming. He looked surprised.

"Lessons like Dorla has?" he said.

"Not quite like Dorla's," said Mother. "Yours will be more simple to start with. But you'll soon be wallowing just as well as her."

"No he won't," I said. "He's too silly to do it properly."

"I am not," said Dilly. "I can be just as good as you."

29

"That's enough of that, you two," said
Mother. "I don't want to hear any more
arguing . . . and can you hurry up now?
I want to get to the office before it
closes."

Dilly was still quiet when we got
home.

"Aren't you excited about your
lessons, Dilly?" said Father. "Once
you've learned how to wallow properly
you can have lots of fun. You'll be able
to go down the mud slide and wallow
where it's deep and warm."

Dilly didn't say anything. He didn't seem to want to talk about The Swamp, or wallowing lessons, at all. Later, when he went to bed, Mother and Father said they thought he might be nervous about having lessons.

"You were scared before your first lesson, weren't you, Dorla?" said Father. "Do you remember? It was a couple of weeks before you really started to enjoy it."

I did remember being scared. I wasn't frightened of the other little dinosaurs in my class, or the mud, or the teacher. I was scared that I would have to do something that I didn't like.

Mother and Father said they thought Dilly was scared because he didn't know what happened in a wallowing lesson. They asked me to tell him so that he would understand there was nothing to

31

be frightened of. I said I would.

But it was Dilly who asked me first. I was in my room reading *The Wind in the Giant Ferns* when I heard someone coming up the stairs, stamp, stamp, stamp, and along the landing, stamp, stamp, STAMP! Then my door flew open and went BANG! against the wall.

It was Dilly, and he had his I'm-going-to-ask-you-a-very-important-question look on his face.

"Dorla," he said.

"What, Dilly?"

"Er . . . well . . . what do you actually *do* in a swamp wallowing lesson?"

I told him that he wasn't to be frightened, because the teacher was very nice and would look after him. But I couldn't remember exactly what the very young dinosaurs did in the baby class . . . so I thought I'd tell Dilly about all the exciting things he would be able to do once he could wallow well enough to go into a class like mine.

I told him how great it was when we jumped in where the mud was really deep. I said that sometimes we went right under the mud, and came up coughing and spluttering. And last week, I said, my friend Doni didn't come up for ages. The teacher thought she'd lost her, but she came up in the end, and only cried for a little while . . .

It was funny, though. Dilly didn't look very excited by what I was telling him. In fact, he looked even more worried when he left my room . . . I couldn't understand it.

A few days later, when it was nearly time to go to The Swamp for his first lesson, Mother asked him if he would like to help pack his things.

"See, Dilly?" she said. "Here's the new outfit I bought for you. It looks really good, doesn't it? You're going to be the best-dressed little dinosaur in The Swamp in these stripes . . ."

"I won't," said Dilly. "I'll look stupid."

"Don't be like that, Dilly," said Mother. "Here's your towel, and your mud wings to help you float . . . and I've packed some Crispy Fern Flakes and a

carton of pineapple juice, too. You can
have a snack straight after you come out.
You'll probably be really hungry by
then."

"I won't," said Dilly. I thought
Mother was sure to tell him off for being
so sulky, but she didn't. When Father
took Dilly out to the dino-car, she told
me she thought he was still nervous
about his lesson.

When we got there, Mother took Dilly out of the changing room to the side of The Swamp. There he had to line up with the other little dinosaurs in his class. He looked very small, and very frightened.

The teacher said hello, and started asking them their names. As she moved down the line towards Dilly, I had a feeling I knew what was going to happen. Dilly had the look on his face he usually does when he's winding up to let loose a 150-mile-per-hour super-scream . . .

The next moment I heard a scream, a very loud scream . . . but it didn't sound like the usual scream Dilly lets rip.

Dilly was still standing there with his
mouth open . . . but there was no noise
coming from it. The scream was coming
from the little dinosaur next to him. And

Dilly was looking at him as if he couldn't
believe what he was hearing.

The little dinosaur didn't stop
screaming for a long time. He wouldn't
get into the mud, either, with the other
little dinosaurs. He kicked and
struggled, and tried to bite the teacher.
He held on to the diving branch on the
giant fern, and wouldn't let go.

The other little dinosaurs all behaved
very well, though – even Dilly. They got
into the mud and did what the teacher
asked them, and the only problem was

that they kept looking at the naughty little dinosaur when they should have been looking at the teacher. His father finally had to carry him away under his arm, the way Father has to carry Dilly sometimes when he's being naughty.

Once he'd gone, there was no trouble at all.

"Well, Dilly," said Mother after the lesson was over, "did you enjoy that? It looked like lots of fun."

Dilly didn't seem to be listening to Mother, though.

"Why did that little dinosaur scream so much?" he said.

"I think he was scared, Dilly," said Mother. "Weren't you when you arrived today?"

"No, Mother," said Dilly. "I wasn't scared at all."

Mother and Father said later they thought Dilly had been so interested in that other little dinosaur that he'd forgotten to be frightened himself.

"About that naughty dinosaur," I heard him say to Mother at bedtime.

"Do you think he's more naughty than me?"

"Not quite, Dilly," Mother laughed. "I don't think anyone could be as naughty as you."

Dilly didn't say anything. But Mother said he was smiling when he went to sleep . . .

IV.   DILLY AND THE CHRISTMAS
PRESENTS

Christmas is my favourite time of the
year. It's really terrific.

The only trouble with Christmas is
. . . Dilly. He gets so excited that he
almost always does something he
shouldn't. And last year, he was
naughtier than ever.

It started at breakfast one day.
Mother said she was thinking of doing
some Christmas shopping. As soon as
Dilly heard Mother say 'Christmas', he

looked up and said something. But none of us could understand a word.

"Dilly Dinosaur," said Father, "if I've told you once, I've told you a thousand times – you must never speak with your mouth full!"

Dilly chewed very fast, then swallowed with a gulp.

"Is it Christmas tomorrow?" he said. Mother smiled.

"No, Dilly," she said. "But it won't be long now."

"Does that mean Dino Claus will be coming soon?" Dilly said.

"Of course it doesn't, silly Dilly," I said. "Everyone knows that Dino Claus only comes on the night before Christmas."

"Now, now, Dorla," said Father. "Don't be mean to your little brother."

"Tell us, Father," said Dilly. "Tell us

about Dino Claus!'' He was very excited.
Father said that Dino Claus lives in
The Great Swamp with lots of helpers.
They make the toys he takes to young
dinosaurs all over the world. Father also
explained how Dino Claus rides in a
special sleigh pulled by six magic
dinosaurs who can fly.

"You look a little confused, Dilly," said Mother.

"Is it a very, very, very, very big sleigh, Father?" Dilly said.

"It's quite big," said Father, "but not *that* big."

"So how does Dino Claus get all the toys in it?" asked Dilly. "You told us the other day that there are millions and billions and zillions of young dinosaurs in the world."

Father laughed.

"I don't know if there are quite that many, Dilly," he said. "But the truth is that Dino Claus only brings the little presents you find in your Christmas stocking on Christmas Day. Mothers and Fathers buy the bigger ones."

I could see that Dilly had his very thoughtful look on his face.

"Father," he said after a while, "do

you and Mother buy Christmas presents for me . . . *before* Christmas Day?"

"Er . . . well . . . yes, Dilly," said Father. "I just said that."

"Well," said Dilly, "what do you do with them then?"

"We hide them away where naughty little dinosaurs won't find them," said Mother. "And you're not to go looking for any presents, either. Dino Claus only brings presents for good little dinosaurs."

"I'll be good, Mother," said Dilly. "I really will."

Anyway, soon it really began to feel like Christmas. We started to get lots of Christmas cards, and Dilly didn't do anything bad for several days.

But as Christmas got closer and closer, he began to act very strangely. Once or twice I found him doing some very odd things. I saw him looking under a rug and peering into a vase, which he nearly knocked over. I caught him looking under bushes in the garden, and behind the giant fern, and in other odd places.

But when I asked him what he was doing, he just said . . . "Oh, nothing," and walked away. And whenever

Mother or Father were around, he didn't do any looking at all.

Then one day, Mother found Dilly in her bedroom.

"Dilly Dinosaur," I heard her say, "what are you doing? Why have you opened that drawer?"

"Er . . . I was looking for a sweater, Mother," he said. He'd gone quite green with embarrassment.

Mother looked rather cross.

"Now you know very well that *your* sweaters are in *your* drawer in *your* room, Dilly," she said. "I hope you weren't looking for any Christmas presents . . . were you?"

"Oh no, Mother," said Dilly. He went a little greener.

"Ummm . . . " said Mother. She didn't look as if she believed him. "Well just make sure you don't," she said.

"I will, Mother," said Dilly. "Er, I mean, I won't."

The next day was the day before Christmas Eve. We were going to see Grandmother and Grandfather. But when Mother was getting Dilly ready to go out, she began to sniff.

"Whatever is that smell?" she said. Father and I started to sniff too. Sniff, sniff, we all went – all of us, that is, except Dilly. And that was because the smell seemed to be coming from . . . *him*.

"Dilly Dinosaur," said Father. "What have you been up to?"

"Me, Father?" said Dilly. "I haven't done anything. I could see that he was beginning to go a little green and hot.

"Have you been touching things you're not allowed to?" said Father. "Things in the bathroom?" Dilly said nothing.

"Right," said Father. "Unless you tell me what you've done by the time I've counted to five, Dilly, you're going to be in a lot of trouble. One . . . two . . . three . . . four . . ."

Father never made it to five. Dilly opened his mouth, but all that came out was . . . an ultra-special, 150-mile-per-hour super-scream, the one that makes Father run outside and slam the door,

Mother and I dive under the table, and all the baubles on the Christmas tree explode.

When Dilly had calmed down, Mother and Father told him off. It turned out that Dilly had been looking for any

Christmas presents Father had hidden in his drawer – and he'd found one, all wrapped up. Dilly thought it was for him, but it was a bottle of perfume

Father had bought for Mother. Dilly had unwrapped it, taken the top off . . . and spilt it, mostly over himself.

Father was cross, and said that Dilly had been very, very naughty.

"You'll have to have a bath, too," he said. "You can't go out smelling like that."

But Mother said there wasn't time. We had promised to be at Grandmother and Grandfather's house by eight o'clock, and it was nearly that now.

Father gave Dilly a quick wash, but Dilly still smelt of perfume when we left. As soon as we arrived, Grandmother and Grandfather asked what the smell was. They laughed when Mother and Father told them.

But Dilly didn't laugh. He looked fed up. He also looked a little worried.

"Father," he said that night at bedtime, "will I still get some presents from Dino Claus now that I've been naughty?"

"There's still a whole day to go," said Father. "It's Christmas Eve tomorrow, and if you're good all day, Dino Claus *might* still bring you some presents . . . "

Dilly was very helpful and well-behaved on Christmas Eve. Father hung up our Christmas stockings, and said that the sooner we were asleep, the

sooner it would be Christmas Day.

He was right. When I woke up, my stocking was full of lovely Christmas presents . . . and so was Dilly's. All our presents from Mother and Father were round the Christmas tree, and we had a wonderful time opening them.

Dilly was so excited and pleased with his presents that he promised he would

be good for a whole year, right up to
next Christmas!

But I'm not sure whether Dilly *can* be
good for a whole year.

Do you think he can?

DILLY AND THE TIGER

1. DILLY AT THE TOYSHOP

One Saturday, we had to go to the Shopping Cavern. As soon as we arrived, Dilly started yelling and bouncing up and down.

"Dilly!" said Mother. "Will you please stop doing that! What do you think you are, a yo-yo?"

"But Mother," said Dilly. "Look! A toyshop!"

He was right. There *was* a toyshop, a brand new one. He ran up to it and

pressed his snout against the window.

"Can we go in, Mother?" he said.

"I suppose so," said Mother, with a sigh. "But we're not buying anything . . . Dilly, are you listening?"

Dilly had already run into the shop. As soon as he saw all the amazing toys inside, he stood absolutely still, his mouth open and his eyes as wide as swamp bubbles.

"*Wow*!" he said. There were so many toys, we didn't know where to start looking.

"Come on, you two," Father said. "We haven't got all day."

I went over to a big display of dinosaur dolls with Father. The one I liked best was Dindy. You can buy lots of different clothes to dress her up in, and special ribbons for her tail. A Dindy doll costs quite a lot of money, but Father said that if I saved my pocket money, it wouldn't be too long before I could buy one.

After a while, Father said we'd better find the others. They were in another part of the shop, looking at a display of toy dino-cars, the sort you sit in and pedal. Dilly was sitting inside a beautiful green and yellow one.

"Come on, Dilly," said Father. "It's time to go."

"But I don't want to go, Father, I like

it here, broomm, broomm, beep beep!"
said Dilly. "And I want this toy
dino-car."

"Now, Dilly," said Father. "Mother
said we weren't going to buy any toys
today, and besides, a toy dino-car is very
expensive."

Dilly reached into the pocket of his
dungarees, dug down deep, and pulled
out something very small. It was a shiny
coin.

"It's all right, Father," he said with a
smile. "I've got some money."

"I'm afraid that's not enough, Dilly," said Father.

Dilly's smile vanished.

"Well, how much is enough?" he said. He looked quite cross and sulky.

"More than you can afford at the moment, I'm afraid," said Father. "Now come along . . . ."

"But I want it," said Dilly, in a small, whiny voice.

"You could save up for it," I said. Dilly didn't understand, so I explained how I wasn't going to spend my pocket money when I got it every week. Instead, I was going to save it so that I

could buy a Dindy doll.

"That's a good idea, Dorla," said Father, who kept looking at his watch. "But can we talk about it later, *after* we've been to the supermarket?"

The next day, I asked Mother and Father if I could earn some extra pocket money by helping around the house. That way, I would be able to save up for my Dindy doll more quickly. Mother and Father said it was OK, so long as I really did help.

Dilly asked if he could do the same.

"I'm going to save up and buy the toy dino-car," he said.

"That might take too long, Dilly," said Mother. "A toy dino-car is very expensive."

"I don't mind how long it takes, Mother," said Dilly.

"Well, we'll see . . . " said Mother. I

didn't think he would help. But he did.
Usually he won't get himself ready in the
morning, but every day that week he got
up and washed and dressed himself,
without being told to. He kept his room

tidy, helped to set the table and clear it
after meals, and watered the fern plants
in the garden.

At the end of the week, Mother and
Father said they were very pleased with
what we'd done, and gave us both our
extra pocket money.

We did the same the next week, and
the week after that Mother gave Dilly a
jar to save his money in, and soon he
had quite a few shiny coins. Almost
every day, he asked her to count it for
him. Some days he even asked her to
weigh it on the kitchen scales.

"Have I got enough yet for the toy
dino-car, Mother?" he said one day.

"That dino-car costs a lot, Dilly," she
said. Just at that moment there was a
knock on the door.

"But how much have I got?" said
Dilly.

"What, Dilly?" said Mother, as she

went to the door. It was the post dinosaur. "I can't remember now," she said. "Quite a lot, anyway."

Dilly didn't say anything. He just smiled.

The next day was shopping day again, and we went to the Shopping Cavern as usual. Dilly insisted on bringing his jar of money with him, and when we arrived at the toyshop, he ran straight in.

"Dilly! Come back this instant!" called Father, and we all ran in after him.

It didn't take long to find Dilly. He was sitting in the beautiful green and yellow toy dino-car, making lots of noise and crashing it into the other ones on display.

"Dilly!" said Father, in a very cross voice. "This isn't a racing track! Stop that immediately!"

"It's OK, Father," said Dilly, with a great big smile, "it's going to be my dino-car now. I've saved up my money, so I can buy it today."

"I'm sorry, Dilly," said Father, "but I don't think you can."

Dilly looked confused.

"But Mother said the dino-car costs a lot," said Dilly. "And she said I had a lot of money, too."

"But you still haven't got enough, Dilly," said Mother. "Look . . . I'll count it for you. Then you'll see."

Mother took Dilly's money jar over to the cash desk. She emptied it, and the nice dinosaur who serves you helped her to count it. There wasn't enough to buy the toy dino-car.

"I'm sorry, Dilly," said Mother. "You *have* got enough to buy something less expensive, though."

"But I want the toy dino-car," said Dilly, in a very cross voice. "And I don't want anything else." He sat there, arms folded, looking very sulky.

The dinosaur from behind the cash desk came over.

"You can always sit in the dino-car when you come to the toy shop," she said with a smile. "And in the meantime you can keep saving."

Dilly didn't say anything. He just stuck his tongue out at her.

"Dilly!" said Father, in a very cross voice. "Don't be so rude! If you're not out of there by the time I count to three,

65

you're going to be in big trouble. One
. . . two . . . "

Father never got to number three.
Dilly opened his mouth . . . and let rip
with a 150-mile-per-hour, ultra-special
super-scream, the kind that sends us

diving for cover and makes everyone
else run out of the shop.

His bad behaviour didn't end there,
either. Even when he'd stopped
screaming, he wouldn't get out of the toy
dino-car. He held on to it as tight as he

could, and kicked and swished his tail
around. Father had to prise his paws off,
and as he was struggling to carry him out
of the shop, they bumped into a big
display of building boulders and knocked
it right over.

Of course, Mother and Father were very, very cross with Dilly. They told him off, and as soon as we got home, they sent him straight to his room without any supper.

Later, after Dilly said he was sorry, Mother and Father had a talk with him. They said it took far too long to save up for big things like the dino-car. It was the sort of toy you got for Christmas, or your birthday – but only if you were a good little dinosaur.

Dilly looked thoughtful for a moment.

"If I'm *really* good," he said, "could we have Christmas or my birthday early?"

Mother and Father laughed.

2.   DILLY AND THE TIGER

One day Dilly and I were watching a programme about mammoths on TV. As soon as it was over, Dilly jumped up and started pretending to be one.

"Hey, look out!" I said.

It was too late. Dilly crashed into the little table where Mother puts our drinks. The cups went flying, and there was pineapple juice all over the rug.

Mother heard the noise and came in.

"Dilly!" she said. "You're like a

sabre-tooth tiger in a china shop."

Dilly said he was sorry. Mother mopped up the mess while we picked up the cups and straightened the table.

"Mother," said Dilly when everything was tidy, "what's a sabre-tooth tiger?"

"Well, Dilly," said Mother, "it's a large, fierce creature with two very big teeth . . . I think we might have a picture of one in a book, somewhere . . ."

Mother found the book, and showed it to Dilly. It explained how sabre-tooth tigers hunted all sorts of animals, even mammoths. Dilly sat quietly listening.

"Mother," he said, after a while, "do sabre-tooth tigers eat . . . dinosaurs?"

"No, Dilly," she laughed. "In fact, quite a few dinosaurs have them as pets."

Dilly seemed quite impressed. The next day, he got Mother to make him some big teeth out of paper so that he could pretend to be a sabre-tooth.

"You're a big, woolly mammoth," he growled at me later from the back of an armchair, "and I'm going to . . . EAT YOU UP!"

He jumped with a roar, but I got out of the way . . . and he landed right on top of the little table again. There was a great crash. Our cups were broken, and so was the table.

Mother was really angry. She didn't believe it was just Dilly's fault, so she told us both off and sent us to our rooms.

I was cross, because that meant I had to miss a programme I really like, *Dinosaur Street*. So as we were going upstairs, I said I hoped a sabre-tooth tiger would come to our house soon and gobble Dilly up, tail and all.

"But Mother said they don't eat dinosaurs," said Dilly, sticking his tongue out.

"She only said that because she didn't want to frighten you," I said. "They do really, and their favourite meal is a juicy little dinosaur, just like you!"

...on toast?
...lightly boiled?
...roasted?

Dilly didn't say anything. He went into his room, and I didn't think any more about it.

Later, we both came downstairs and

said we were sorry. Mother was telling us we weren't ever to be so naughty again, when the dino-phone rang.

"Hello?" said Mother. "Oh yes . . . of course . . . how wonderful! . . . Bye!"

She put the dino-phone down.

"Well, Dilly," she said with a smile, "that was Dixie's mother. She's bringing Dixie over tomorrow."

Dilly started bouncing up and down with excitement. Dixie is his best friend, and there's nothing he likes better than playing with her.

"Oh yes, I nearly forgot," said Mother. "Dixie will have a surprise for you tomorrow, too."

"What sort of surprise, Mother?" said Dilly.

"Ah, it won't be a surprise if I tell you, will it?" said Mother with a smile. "You'll find out tomorrow."

The next day, Dilly couldn't wait for Dixie to arrive. At last we heard footsteps coming up the path, and a knock on the door. There were some other strange noises, too – a sort of growling. Dilly didn't seem to notice anything, though.

Mother opened the door, and Dilly rushed forward.

"Hi, Dixie, where's the sur . . . " he started to say, but then he stopped. He stood there, with his mouth open, looking at what we could all see on the doorstep.

A great big, furry, stripy, growling . . . sabre-tooth tiger.

Standing next to it was Dixie. She was holding a lead which was attached to the tiger's collar, and she had a huge smile on her face.

"Surprise!" she said. "Do you like my

tiger, Dilly? His name's Titan."

Dilly didn't say anything.

Dixie told us all about her new pet.
She said that even though he looked
very big, he was still only a cub, and that
he would get much bigger and stronger.

"Why don't you take him out into the
garden, Dixie?" said Mother. "You'll
enjoy that, won't you, Dilly? Dilly!
Where are you?"

Dilly had gone upstairs. He said he
didn't want to go in the garden, either.
Mother said she thought he was
probably a little jealous of Titan, and
asked me to play with Dixie instead.

It was fun playing with Titan, but very tiring. At last he lay down for a sleep. Mother asked me to try and get Dilly to come out of his room, so I went indoors. I knocked on his door.

"Come on, Dilly," I said. "You can't sit in there all day."

There was no answer.

"Dixie will probably have to go home soon," I said. "I've been playing with Titan, and he's gone to sleep."

There was still no answer.

"Suit yourself," I said, and went downstairs.

A few minutes later, Dilly came down too. He acted very strangely, though. He kept looking through all the doors and over his shoulder.

"Oh, hello, Dilly," said Mother when she saw him. "We were just going to have a drink and a snack. Would you like something?"

"Er . . . what?" said Dilly, looking round, quickly. "Oh, yes please."

Mother gave him a packet of crispy fern stalks and a cup of pineapple juice.

"We're all having ours in the garden," she said. "Are you coming out too? It's a lovely day."

"Er . . . no, Mother," he said.

So Dilly stayed inside. We sat under the giant fern in the garden, near Titan.

After a while, he yawned, stretched, and stood up. He trotted round the garden for a while, and then he went indoors.

"I wonder why Dilly's acting so strangely . . . " Mother began to say,

when all of a sudden, there was the
sound of . . . an ultra-special, 150-mile-
per-hour super-scream, the sort that
makes us all run into the house to see
what's wrong.

We found Dilly standing in a corner.
He had both his eyes shut tight, and
looked terrified.

Titan was standing in front of Dilly.
As we watched, his big red tongue came
out and licked Dilly's snout with a loud,
rasping noise . . . slurrrppp!

"What on earth is the matter, Dilly?"
said Mother.

"Titan . . . tried . . . to . . . eat me!"
he said, and burst into tears.

"There, there, Dilly," she said. "He was only trying to be friendly. Anyway, don't you remember what I said? Tigers don't eat dinosaurs."

"But Dorla told me they did," sniffed Dilly.

"Oh, did she now?" said Mother. "Dorla . . . where do you think you're going? I want to have a word with you . . ."

Of course, Mother was very cross with me. She said it wasn't very nice to try and frighten someone, whether they'd made you miss your favourite TV programme or not. I said I was sorry, and that I wouldn't do it ever again.

It took ages to calm Dilly down, and even when he was quiet, he still didn't want to go near Titan. It was Dixie who made everything all right in the end, though. She told Dilly Titan was sorry he had upset him, and that he wanted to be his friend.

Titan was lying down in front of Dilly, his head on his paws, and he did seem to be saying he was sorry. Dilly gave him a very careful look . . . and then he patted his head once, very quickly.

But by the time Dixie went home, Dilly was very friendly with Titan. In fact, they were so friendly that Dilly was having rides on Titan's back, and didn't want him to go.

At bedtime that evening, Dilly charged around pretending to be a tiger. And then I heard him ask Mother if we could have a tiger, just like Titan.

"I don't know about that, Dilly," I heard her say. "I think one tiger in the family is quite enough!"

3. DILLY AND THE CONTRARY DAY

"Mother," said Dilly at breakfast yesterday, "will you play with me today?"

Now if there's one thing Dilly really enjoys, it's having Mother or Father play with him. But they don't often have the time.

"I'm afraid not, Dilly," said Mother.

"But why?" said Dilly.

"I've got too much to do," said Mother. "Your father and I are having some friends round for dinner this evening, so we're going to be very busy."

"But it's not fair," said Dilly. "You never play with me."

"I'm sorry, Dilly," said Mother, "but today I just can't. Besides, I was hoping that you and Dorla would help me. Wouldn't you like to?"

"No I would not!" shouted Dilly. Then he got down from the table and stomped away, STAMP! STAMP! STAMP!

Mother was a little cross with Dilly, and told him off. She also said he had to put the toys back in our big toy cupboard. The night before he had got most of them out, and then left them on the floor at bedtime.

Dilly didn't say anything. But I could tell he wasn't very happy.

Mother started tidying up the downstairs rooms. She got the vacuum cleaner out, but it didn't seem to be working properly.

"The fern pod probably needs changing," said Mother. "There's a new one in the store cupboard, Dorla. Run along and fetch it for me, will you?"

The store cupboard is in the same room as the big toy cupboard, along with a few other cupboards and boxes where we keep all sorts of things.

When I got there, I pushed the door, but it wouldn't open. I pushed again, harder, and it opened a tiny crack.

I peeked through . . . and I could hardly believe what I saw.

"What's taking so long?"

It was Mother. I told her I couldn't open the door, and she began to look worried.

"Is Dilly in there?" she said.

"Er . . . yes, Mother," I said, "but I think . . ."

Mother didn't listen. She just pushed the door as hard as she could. There was a crunching, cracking sound, and the door moved back slowly, until it was half open.

And there before us was the biggest mess you've ever seen.

Dilly hadn't tidied his toys away. Instead, he'd got them all out and piled them in a great heap. Then he must have emptied the other cupboards and boxes, too, and put everything from them on top of the mound of toys. It was the mound that had been blocking the door.

"Dilly!" said Mother, in a shocked voice, "what have you got to say for yourself?"

Dilly didn't say anything. He just stuck his tongue out.

Of course, Mother was very, very cross. She was even more cross when she found out that the crunching, cracking sound had been the spare fern pod for the vacuum cleaner breaking when she opened the door.

It was the only one we had, too.

"I'll never get everything done today!" she said. She told Dilly off again, and sent him straight to his room.

It took ages to clear up the mess he had made. After we'd done it, Mother looked at her watch.

"Oh my," she said, "if I don't get those swamp moss rolls in the oven soon they won't be ready in time!"

Later, at lunchtime, Mother said Dilly could come out of his room if he was sorry and promised to behave. He said he would, but I didn't think he really meant it.

I was right, too. Things went from bad to worse. In the afternoon, Mother said she was going to do the upstairs rooms while Father started preparing the rest of the dinner.

"So you two can go outside and play in the garden," she said. "I don't want you under my feet while I'm busy."

But Dilly, of course, had other ideas.

"Can you play with me now, Mother?" he said.

"I've already told you once I can't, Dilly," she said. "Now be a good little dinosaur and do what you're told for once."

"I won't!" said Dilly. "I don't want to play in the smelly old garden," he said, looking really sulky.

Mother looked even more cross than ever.

"Dilly, why are you being so contrary today?" she said. "I think if you say 'No' or 'I don't want to' again today, I'll scream."

Dilly opened his mouth to say something. For a second, I thought he was going to do what he usually does when he can't get his own way . . . but he didn't. He closed his mouth again, and we both went outside to play.

I didn't stay outside for long, though. Dilly was in a very bad mood, and kept saying horrible things. So I decided to go indoors.

"Just make sure you wipe your feet before you come in, Dorla," Father said. "The garden's a little muddy, and we don't want the floors to get all dirty after we've just cleaned them."

I wiped my feet carefully, and went upstairs. Mother had finished tidying, and said that she was going to start getting herself ready.

"I've bought a new dress to wear this evening," she said. "What do you think of it, Dorla?"

Mother got the new dress out of her wardrobe to show me. It was a beautiful swamp green, with yellow stripes. I said it was lovely.

"I'm going to have a bath now,"

Mother said. "You could go and help
your father with the cooking, Dorla. Tell
him those swamp moss rolls have got to
come out of the oven at six o'clock, or
they'll be spoilt."

I said I would.

Mother went into the bathroom, and I
went downstairs to help Father. It didn't
take long to finish everything, and then
there wasn't much else to do. So Father

decided to have a shower, and I went to my room.

We had both forgotten about Dilly.

About half an hour later, I heard them come out of the bathroom.

"Oh, no!" I heard Mother say. I went to see what was the matter.

Mother and Father were on the landing, looking down at the carpet. There were small, muddy footprints all over it. They came up the stairs and went in the direction of Mother and Father's bedroom.

"Dilly . . . " Mother said, and opened her bedroom door.

The bedroom was in a terrible mess. Someone had been drawing pictures with Mother's make-up on the dressing table mirror. A lot of the drawers were open, with everything hanging out of them. There were muddy footprints

everywhere, too, even on the bed.

And that's where Dilly was standing. In fact, he was bouncing up and down on Mother's new dress, which was under his feet, all screwed up and covered in mud.

Mother was *furious*.

"Dilly Dinosaur," she said from between clenched teeth, "get off that bed *immediately*!"

"No! I will not," he said, and stuck his tongue out at her. She was about to say something when she started to sniff.

"What's that smell?" she said.

"Oh no!" said Father, rushing out. "The swamp moss rolls! They're burning!"

Mother had a very strange look on her face. She shut her eyes, opened her mouth . . . and out came something that sounded just like one of Dilly's ultra-special, 150-mile-per-hour super-screams.

Dilly and I dived for cover, and we didn't come out until Mother had stopped.

Dilly was in a lot of trouble. Father was so cross he actually spanked him, and that's something he hardly ever does. He was also sent to bed without any supper.

The next day, Mother and Father said their evening hadn't turned out too badly in the end. Dilly looked very ashamed, and said he was sorry.

For the rest of that day, he kept giving Mother funny looks.

"Mother," I heard him say at last, "you've got a very loud scream."

"Now you know where you get it from," she said, and winked.

Dilly just smiled.

4. DILLY AND THE BIRTHDAY TREAT

Last week, Dilly asked Father if it was his birthday soon.

"It's not too far away now, Dilly," said Father. "About a month or so."

"Yippee!" shouted Dilly. "And can I have a birthday treat this year, like Dorla did for *her* birthday?"

For my birthday this year, instead of giving me an ordinary party, Mother and Father had taken me on an outing with some of my friends from school. We went swamp wallowing, and we had a wonderful time.

"I don't know," said Father. "You're still a little young for an outing like that."

"It's not fair," said Dilly. "I want to go swamp wallowing with my friends, just like Dorla did."

"I suppose it might be all right," said Father. "You *have* been doing very well in your swamp wallowing lessons."

"Yes, I have," said Dilly, with a big smile. "I can almost wallow a whole width now."

"But we'll only be able to take a few of your friends," said Father.

"That's OK, Father," said Dilly. "We could take Dixie, and Doopa, and a couple of others."

"Well . . . that should be OK, Dilly," said Father. "I'll get everything arranged."

"And can we go to MacDinosaur's for lunch that day, too?" said Dilly.

"I suppose so," said Father, with a sigh.

Later, Mother and Father asked me if I would go along. They said they would need my help to look after Dilly and his little friends. I said I would.

From then on, Dilly spent most of his time thinking about his outing.

"What time will my friends arrive on my birthday, Father?" he would ask.

"What, Dilly? I think we've asked them to come at about twelve on the invitation."

"And will we go straight to MacDinosaur's?"

"I should think so, Dilly," Father would sigh.

"Good," Dilly would say. "Now I'll sit between Dixie and Derri, and I'll have a

Triple-Dipple Bronto-burger and an extra thick milk shake . . . "

Dilly wanted to plan what his friends would have for lunch, what games they would play in the dino-car on the way to the swamp, who would get in the swamp first (that was him), and who would get out last (that was him, too). And he kept repeating "It's going to be the BEST BIRTHDAY EVER."

Finally, it was the morning of Dilly's birthday. And didn't we know it!

I was woken up very, very early by the noise coming from Dilly's room. It sounded as if he was pulling things out of his drawers. Then I heard him go into Mother and Father's room, so I went in too.

Dilly was dressed in his swamp wallowing outfit. He even had his mud wings on, although they weren't blown

up, and the mask and goggles Mother
and Father had bought him for doing so
well in his lessons.

"Yippee!" he shouted, and jumped on
the bed. Mother and Father were
snuggled deep down under the
bedclothes. I heard Father groan.

"Dilly," he said, "have you any idea
what time it is?"

"Yes, Father," Dilly laughed. "IT'S
BIRTHDAY TIME! AND IT'S GOING
TO BE THE BEST BIRTHDAY
EVER!"

And then he started to bounce up and down on the bed. As you can probably tell, Dilly was rather excited.

Dilly's present from Mother and Father was a Superdinosaur costume, and he was really pleased with it. I gave him a packet of candied fern flakes, and a card I'd made. Mother said that Grandma and Grandpa would come later with their present, after we got back from the outing. Dilly said he couldn't wait.

"Come on, Dilly," said Father when he got up to make breakfast. "Get your clothes on. You can't go around in your wallowing outfit all morning."

"But I don't want to get dressed, Father," said Dilly. "I want to go on my outing *now*."

"It isn't time to go yet," said Father. "Your friends won't be here until twelve, and it's only eight o'clock."

I could see Dilly wasn't very happy about that.

"Why don't you put your Superdinosaur costume on?" said Father, quickly. "I'm sure Dorla will help you . . . *won't* you, Dorla?"

"I suppose so," I said. "Come on, Dilly . . . "

After breakfast, Father said he was relying on me to help keep Dilly calm. He said that Dilly was already over-excited, and that if he got any worse, there was bound to be trouble. I said I would do my best.

The morning dragged by for all of us.
Dilly soon got bored with playing at
being Superdinosaur. And after that he
was a real pest. He kept asking what
time it was and whether his friends
would arrive soon.

At last it was twelve o'clock, and there
was a knock on the door. Dilly raced to
the door shouting, "IT'S THE BEST
BIRTHDAY EVER!" It was Doopa,
and Dilly's other friends came soon
after.

"Can we go now, Father?" said Dilly.
He started to bounce up and down.
"Can we go? Please? *Please*?"

We left the dino-car in the
parking cave, and set off towards
MacDinosaur's. But when we got there
it looked very strange. The lights weren't
on, and there were no people inside.
Mother tried the doors, but they

wouldn't open. There was a little sign on them. Father leant forward to read it.

"Closed . . . for . . . re-decoration," he read out, slowly. "Oh dear," he said, in an embarrassed voice. "I'm sorry, Dilly, but it looks as if we won't be able to have lunch at MacDinosaur's after all."

Dilly looked really disappointed. He loves going to MacDinosaur's. His snout started to wobble the way it always does when he's going to cry.

"But it's my birthday," he said, quietly.

"Never mind, Dilly," said Father with a smile. "We can have something to eat in the cafeteria at the swamp. You'd like that, wouldn't you?"

Dilly cheered up straight away.

'What did you say today was going to be?" asked Father.

"It's going to be THE BEST BIRTHDAY EVER!" shouted Dilly.

So we all piled back into the dino-car and went off to the swamp.

But when we got there, we found that it was very crowded. We had to park the dino-car a long way away, and it took ages to get into the cafeteria. And then there was a huge queue to get into the swamp itself.

It was absolutely packed. There was hardly room to do any wallowing at all,

and Dilly's friends didn't like all the
noise, and the big dinosaurs jumping in.
Father tried to make sure Dilly had a
good time, but it was impossible. Then,
just fifteen minutes or so after we'd got
in, the attendant said it was time to get
out.

"That's it, I'm afraid, Dilly," said
Father. "We have to go home now."

"But it's my birthday!" said Dilly,
with a sob . . . and then he let rip with
an ultra-special, 150-mile-per-hour
super-scream, the sort that empties the
swamp in seconds.

But it didn't make any difference. We still had to get out.

Poor Dilly cried all the way home, and he still didn't look very happy, even when Father brought out his cake and

we sang Happy Birthday to him.

A few minutes later, there was a knock on the door. It was Grandma and Grandpa . . . and they had brought Dilly an *enormous* present.

"Well, Dilly," said Grandpa. "What do you think this is?"

Everyone stopped stuffing themselves with cake and looked. Dilly didn't say anything. He just ripped off the paper as quickly as he could. And there before him was . . . the beautiful green and yellow toy dino-car he had seen in the toyshop ages ago. And then he smiled for the first time since we'd stood outside MacDinosaur's.

"So are you having a good birthday, Dilly?" Grandpa asked him.

Dilly thought for a while, and then looked at his new toy.

"I am now, Grandpa," he said, with a smile. "IT'S THE BEST BIRTHDAY EVER!"

DILLY AND THE GHOST

DILLY GOES TO THE BEACH

At breakfast yesterday morning, Mother and Father gave us a wonderful surprise.

'How would you two like to go to the beach today?' Father said.

Dilly looked at me, and I looked at Dilly. And we both said . . .

'Hooray!'

I was glad, but Dilly was *really* pleased. If there's one thing he enjoys almost more than anything else, it's a trip to the beach. He started jumping up

109

and down with excitement.

'Can we go now?' he said. 'Now! Now! Now!'

'Whoa there, Dilly,' said Father, 'will you calm down a little? You look as if someone's set your tail on fire. We won't be going anywhere if you behave like that.'

Dilly stopped jumping up and down. I could see he wanted to go to the beach very much.

'That's better,' said Father. 'We all want to enjoy our day at the beach, which means we don't want it spoiled by a naughty little dinosaur. So do you promise you'll be good today?'

'Yes, Father,' said Dilly, with his really-I'm-the-nicest-little-dinosaur-in-the-world-look on his face. 'I promise.'

'Just try your best, anyway,' said Father.

Dilly said he would.

Father made a picnic lunch while Mother, Dilly and I loaded the dino-car. Dilly was very helpful. He seemed determined to prove he could be well behaved. It didn't take long to get to the beach, and when we arrived, we were pleased to see it wasn't crowded.

'Doesn't it look lovely?' said Mother. She was right. Dinosaurs love lying in the sun and splashing in water almost as much as they love mud wallowing, and the beach is perfect for all those things. It's a long curve of fine, golden sand round the bay where the water's always clean and clear. Behind the dunes there

are some giant palm trees, with mud pools nearby.

We found some big, flat rocks to bask on, and Mother put up the parasol so we could have some shade. Father and I unloaded the dino-car. Dilly helped too.

'Come here now, Dilly and Dorla,' said Mother when we'd finished. 'You've got to have some sun cream on.'

I don't mind sun cream. Mother says it stops the sun burning you, and helps your skin turn a lovely dark green colour. Dilly really hates it, though. He says it makes him feel slimy, and the sand sticks to him. So usually he shouts and screams and says he won't have any on. But today he didn't.

'OK, Mother,' he said, and went over to her obediently.

Mother and Father did some basking and reading, and Dilly didn't pester them once. Father went swimming, and tried out a new tail flipper he'd bought. We built a huge sand-castle, with a moat full of water we fetched from the sea in our buckets. Then we collected some shells and seaweed.

The morning went by very quickly. After lunch, we bought ice creams from the little shop at the other end of the beach. Dilly wanted a Frozen Pineapple Delight, but they didn't have any. He didn't complain, even though he loves pineapple juice, and settled for a fern-flavoured Tail Tingler instead.

'I'm very pleased with you today, Dilly,' said Father, as we walked back along the beach. 'You *are* keeping your promise.'

Dilly just smiled. I could hardly

believe it – for once, he was being a real goody two-shoes. A little later, I heard Mother say she thought Dilly was being good because he was enjoying himself so much. Father agreed, and said they shouldn't let him get bored.

So I wasn't surprised when Father asked us to play Find The Treasure. We said yes straight away – it's our favourite beach game. We each get a turn to bury something in the sand, while everyone else keeps their eyes covered, so they don't know what you've chosen or where it is. Then they have to find it.

It was Father's turn first. He buried the tube of sun cream near the rocks, but he'd left so many paw prints in the sand nearby we knew where to start looking as soon as we opened our eyes.

'You're cold,' said Father, laughing. 'Cold . . . warm, warmer — now you're

hot, very hot! You've found it! You must have been cheating! But I'll let you off this time . . . your turn next, Dorla.'

It was lots of fun. We played for ages, right up until it was time to go home.

'Come on, everybody,' said Father at last. 'We'd better start packing everything up.'

'Can I have another turn, Father?' said Dilly. 'Just one more, please?'

'OK, Dilly,' said Father, 'seeing as you've been such a good little dinosaur today. But it will have to be a quick turn. It's getting late.'

We all covered our eyes while Dilly went off to bury something. He called out when he'd finished, and we started looking. We searched, and we searched, but we couldn't find anything. Dilly kept telling us how cold we were. We didn't get warm, not even *once*. Finally Father stopped playing and looked at his watch.

'I'd better start loading some things in the car while you play,' he said. He reached into his pocket. Then he reached into his other pocket. Soon he was looking in all his pockets, and all the bags.

'I can't find the keys to the dino-car,' he said at last. 'I wonder where they can be?' Then he looked at Dilly. 'You haven't buried them, have you, Dilly?'

'No, Father,' said Dilly.

'Are you sure, Dilly? We can't go home without them.'

Dilly said he was sure, but I don't think Father believed him.

'Now, Dilly,' he said, 'you promised to be good today. A game's a game, but we need those keys. Where have you buried them?'

'But I *haven't* buried them, Father,' said Dilly. He was beginning to look a little upset.

Father looked really cross. In fact, his face went dark green, and he started to shout so loudly that most of the other

dinosaurs on the beach turned to look at us.

'You will tell me where you've buried the keys *this instant*!' he shouted. He even stamped his foot like Dilly does when he's having a tantrum.

'Actually, dear, I think . . . ' Mother started to say.

'Not now,' Father snapped. 'Well, Dilly? You're going to be in a lot of trouble unless you tell me. I'm waiting.'

Mother tried again. 'But dear, I really think you ought . . . '

'Not *now*!' Father shouted at her. 'Right, Dilly,' said Father. 'I'll count to three . . .'

Father never even made it to one. Dilly opened his mouth and let rip with an ultra-special, 150-mile-per-hour super-scream. We all dived for cover, and the beach emptied in seconds.

He calmed down in the end, and so did Father. Dilly had only buried one of the shells we'd found, and Mother had been trying to tell Father she thought he'd left the keys in his jacket. It was lying near the rock he'd been basking on. He felt in the pockets . . . and there they were.

Father was very embarrassed, and didn't say much on the way home.

Later, at bedtime, I heard him go into Dilly's room and apologise.

'I'm sorry, Dilly,' he said. 'You did keep your promise today, after all. And you were so good, we've decided to take you and Dorla back to the beach tomorrow. What do you think of that?'

Dilly was quiet for a moment.

'We all want to enjoy our day at the beach, Father,' he said at last. I could hear he was imitating Father's voice! 'That means we don't want it spoiled by you losing your temper again. So do you promise you'll be good?'

'Yes, Dilly,' said Father. 'I promise.'

'Well, just try your best,' said Dilly.

And then they both laughed!

DILLY AND THE LOOSE TOOTH

A few weeks ago one of my teeth came
out. It had been loose for ages, and I put
it under my pillow before I went to
sleep, the way Mother told me to. In the
morning it had gone, and there was a
bright, shiny coin in its place.

'Look, Mother,' I said at breakfast.
'The Tooth Pterodactyl took my tooth
last night, and left me some money.'

'That's nice, Dorla,' said Mother.

'Let me see,' said Dilly. I showed him

the gap where my tooth had been, and the coin. 'But why did your tooth fall out?'

'Don't you know anything, silly Dilly?' I said. 'It's to let my new teeth grow through.'

'Now, now, Dorla,' said Mother. 'That's enough of that. Dilly doesn't understand about teeth coming out because it hasn't happened to him yet. It's quite simple, Dilly . . . '

Mother explained to Dilly all about teeth. She said that baby dinosaurs didn't have any when they hatched from their eggs, but soon grew some. When you were older, these baby teeth got loose and fell out. They were replaced by bigger, stronger teeth, the sort you would need to chew fern stalks with when you were a grown-up dinosaur.

'So when will *my* teeth fall out?'

'I don't know, Dilly,' said Mother. 'I suppose Dorla was a little older than you when she had her first loose tooth. But you might have to wait a bit longer.'

'But that's not fair,' said Dilly. He was beginning to look very grumpy. 'I want one of my teeth to come out, and I want the Tooth Pterodactyl to bring me some money . . . *now*!' Dilly stamped his foot – STAMP! STAMP!

'Now, Dilly,' said Mother. 'The Tooth Pterodactyl only visits good little dinosaurs, the sort who clean their teeth regularly. She doesn't visit little dinosaurs who shout and stamp their feet. So you'll have to be on your best behaviour, won't you?'

Dilly stopped stamping.

'I will be, Mother,' he said, smiling and showing all his teeth.

He was well-behaved for a while, too. He didn't do any of the naughty things he usually does – but he did keep talking about loose teeth and the Tooth Pterodactyl. In fact, hardly a moment went by without Dilly pestering Mother about them. Every time she helped him brush his teeth, he made her check *each one* to see if any were wobbly.

One day Mother got quite cross about it. It was Hallowe'en, and Mother and Father had said I could have a fancy dress party for my friends. I was really excited. But there was lots to do, and Mother was very busy.

'Mother,' said Dilly while she was decorating the table for the party, 'I think one of my teeth is coming out.'

Mother didn't even stop what she was doing to look in Dilly's mouth.

'I'm sure it isn't, Dilly,' she said. 'If I've told you once, I've told you a thousand times, you'll just have to be a little more patient.'

'But, Mother,' said Dilly, 'I want a tooth for the Tooth Pterodactyl.'

'If I could find one to give you, Dilly,' said Mother, 'I would. But I can't at the moment . . . now where did I put those paper plates?'

Dilly looked surprised.

'Does the Tooth Pterodactyl take *any* teeth?' he said. 'And does he give you money for them?'

'What, Dilly?' said Mother. 'I suppose so . . . now will you run along and play?

I've got to get those swamp worm cakes
into the cooker or they'll never be
ready.'

Mother went into the kitchen, and
Dilly stood there for a while with his
thoughtful look on his face. I couldn't
wait around worrying about Dilly,
though. I had to get on and help
Mother.

We finally had everything ready just
before my friends were due to arrive.
Father had carved a giant swamp
mushroom to look like a face and fitted a
candle inside it. We put it in the window
and it looked really spooky.

Mother had made lots of special Hallowe'en food, too. There was a big bowl of steaming marsh-water soup, just like a witch's cauldron, swamp potatoes baked in their jackets, and candied fern stalks in the shape of bat wings.

I still had to get into my witch's costume. Father had helped me make it. There was a big, black pointy hat, a ragged dress, a huge cloak, and a

broomstick to ride on. Mother helped me make up with face paints – we even made some warts out of plasticine. Father said he was scared to look at me!

But I wasn't as scary as some of my friends. Lots of them came dressed as witches, of course, and most of the costumes were terrific. But when Doni arrived, everyone screamed and ran away because he was so terrifying. He was dressed as a . . . *human being*.

My best friend Deena came as Count Dinula, the vampire. She had a black cloak and a bow tie, but best of all, she had these amazing vampire teeth. She had bought them at a joke shop in the Shopping Cavern, and they were so good they looked real.

Dilly couldn't take his eyes off them.

'Your teeth look very sharp, Deena,' he said.

'Urrmmf er, urrmmff . . . ' Deena couldn't speak properly while the teeth were in her mouth. She took them out. 'Don't worry, Dilly,' she said. 'I won't bite you.'

Deena put the teeth down on the table next to her plate. Dilly was sitting next to her, and I could see him staring at them. He looked absolutely fascinated.

I was worried that Dilly would be naughty. He usually is when I have a party, but this time he wasn't. Mother had made him a costume – he was dressed as a little demon. He joined in

all our games, except when we were
Trick or Treating. Mother and Father
said he was too young, even though we
were only going to the houses nearby
with Father.

'You can stay here instead and help
me tidy up, Dilly,' said Mother. I
wondered whether he would make a fuss
– but he didn't. In fact, oddly enough,
he looked really pleased.

Soon it was time for everyone to go
home. It had been a wonderful party.
The only problem was that Deena
couldn't find her vampire teeth. They'd

disappeared. Mother said they would probably turn up in the morning, and that Deena wasn't to worry.

'Come on, Dilly,' said Father when the last guest had gone, 'it's time you were in bed.'

Now usually after he's been doing something exciting, Dilly won't go to bed. But tonight he didn't say a word. In fact he practically *ran* upstairs. Father was really surprised.

'Dilly's acting very strangely tonight,'
he said to Mother when he came
downstairs. 'He got straight into bed, lay
down with his arms by his sides, closed
his eyes and said good night. He didn't
even want any stories.'

Mother said she thought he was
probably very tired after the party, and
we thought no more about it. Soon it
was time for me to go to bed, and I went
straight to sleep too.

The next morning, I hadn't been
awake very long when I heard Dilly
jump out of bed. He was quiet for a
second . . . and then he let rip with an
ultra-special, 150-mile-per-hour super-
scream, the sort that makes everyone
come running to see what's wrong.

Dilly was standing by his bed. The
pillow was on the floor, and where it
should have been we could all see . . .

Deena's vampire teeth! Dilly must have
taken them the night before, and put
them under his pillow for the Tooth
Pterodactyl.

But she hadn't come for them. Dilly
had screamed when he had looked under
his pillow and found the teeth still there
– and no bright, shiny coin.

Of course, Mother gave Dilly quite a
telling off for being deceitful and taking
something that didn't belong to him.
Dilly said he was sorry, and Mother said
she hoped he had learned his lesson.

'The Tooth Pterodactyl will only give you money for your *own* teeth,' I heard her saying later when she was helping Dilly brush his teeth. 'And I don't think you'll have to wait much longer, now, Dilly. I do believe this tooth in the front is a little wobbly. Are you pleased?'

'Yes, Mother,' he said. And he did sound very pleased indeed.

'So am I, Dilly,' said Mother. 'So am I.'

DILLY AND THE X-RAY

Dilly loves riding around on his little dino-trike. He can go really fast on it, too. The trouble is that sometimes he doesn't look where he's going.

Take yesterday, for instance. We were playing in the garden. Dilly was pretending he was Super Dinosaur, and that his dino-trike was rocket powered like one he'd seen in a programme on TV.

'Broomm, broomm!' he shouted.

'You're the evil villain, and I'm coming to get you, Dorla!'

Then he put his head down and pedalled as fast as he could towards me. I got out of the way, but Dilly didn't notice. He shot past and crashed into the giant fern. He flew over the handlebars, bounced off the trunk and lay there on the grass.

Mother and I ran up to him. He was a very pale green, and there was a big bump on his forehead. It seemed to get bigger and bigger before our eyes.

'Are you all right, Dilly?' Mother said. I could see she was very worried.

At first Dilly didn't say anything. But he did open his eyes after a while, and then he started to cry. Mother picked him up and carried him into the house. She put him down on the sofa and had another look at the bump on his head.

Father looked at it too.

Then Mother and Father whispered together. Dilly was beginning to look a little better now. He wasn't quite so pale, and he'd stopped crying. But the bump was very big and had gone a nasty yellow colour.

'My head hurts, Mother,' said Dilly at last.

'I'm not surprised,' said Mother. 'That's quite some bump you've got there . . . I think we ought to take you to the hospital to get it looked at.'

Dilly didn't seem to be worried about going to the hospital. I think that's because one of his favourite games is playing doctors. We've got a toy doctor's outfit, and Dilly really enjoys pretending to be a patient. He especially likes being covered in bandages.

'Will they give me a bandage for my head at the hospital, Mother?' he said when we were in the dino-car on our way there.

'I should think so, Dilly,' said Mother. Dilly smiled for the first time since his accident.

The hospital is very big, with lots of different parts. When we arrived we didn't know where to go. Mother and Father stood in front of a big board covered in signs with arrows pointing in every direction.

'Administration . . . surgery . . . ah, here it is,' said Father. 'Accident and emergency.'

We started walking towards some
doors. Lots of other dinosaurs were
going that way, too. We went into a
large room and up to a desk, where a
nice dinosaur nurse wrote down Dilly's
name and what had happened to him.
She said we would have to wait, so we
found some seats and sat down.

Dilly seemed a lot better now. The
bump was just as big and yellow, but the
rest of his face had got its proper green

colour back. He was looking round at all the other dinosaurs, and he was full of questions, too.

'Father, what does admin . . . admin . . . what does that word mean, and the other one you said?'

Father explained both words. He said that administration was another word for the offices where the people who ran the hospital worked.

'And surgery means having an operation,' he said. 'That's when the doctor has to cut someone open to look in their insides and make them better.'

Dilly looked very thoughtful for a second. He was about to ask another question when he saw something that made him stop and stare.

'Why is that grown-up dinosaur being pushed like a baby, Mother?' he said in a loud voice. He was pointing at an old

dinosaur in a wheelchair. Mother looked
very embarrassed.

'I don't know how many times I've
told you it's rude to point, Dilly. And
keep your voice down,' Mother hissed.
She explained that the old dinosaur was
probably too ill to walk, so he had to
ride in a wheelchair to see the doctor.

'Mother,' he said, 'can I have a ride in a wheelchair? My head still hurts a lot.'

'I think you'll be able to walk when it's your turn to see the doctor, Dilly,' said Mother.

And she was right. There was nothing wrong with Dilly's legs. Soon he was running round the waiting room, staring at all the other dinosaurs and talking to them, climbing on the chairs and pestering the nurse at the desk. Mother told him off and tried to make him sit still. But nobody seemed to mind that much.

We had to wait a long time, but the nurse called out Dilly's name at last. We had to go through a door into a small room. A doctor in a white coat was waiting for us.

She was very nice. She said hello to Dilly, and looked at his bump. She said she thought it was the biggest bump on the head she'd ever seen. Dilly smiled.

'I think a bump like that calls for an X-ray,' said the doctor. She wrote something on a piece of paper, and said we had to go to another part of the hospital. So off we went.

'Father, what's an X-ray?' said Dilly.

'It's a little difficult to explain, Dilly,' said Father. 'Ah . . . here we are. You'll soon find out.'

We went into another room. But this one was full of huge pieces of machinery and a great big table.

'Right, Dilly,' said the doctor. 'Up on the table . . . we're just going to have a look inside your head to make sure everything is all right.'

Dilly shrank back against Mother.

'Come along, Dilly,' said the doctor. 'There's nothing to be worried about.'

Dilly didn't say anything.

'It's OK, Dilly,' said Mother. 'It will be over very quickly.'

I don't think Dilly believed her. He looked at the doctor in the white coat, who stood there smiling.

Then Dilly opened his mouth and . . . that's right, you guessed it, he let rip with a 150-mile-per hour, ultra-special super-scream, the kind that makes doctors jump into cupboards, and shatters the glass test tubes on a table in the corner.

It took ages to calm Dilly down. It turned out that when the doctor said he was going to have a look inside his head, Dilly had thought it meant he was going to have an operation.

'Oh no,' said the doctor, laughing. 'I've got a magic camera that can take pictures of what's inside your head, that's all.'

Dilly was beginning to look quite interested. The doctor showed him other dinosaurs' X-rays.

'So you see, Dilly,' said the doctor, 'we can tell all sorts of things with X-rays. So will you let me take your X-ray now?'

Dilly was quiet for a moment.

'OK,' he said, 'I'll let you do it. But only if you let me have something . . . ' Dilly whispered in the doctor's ear.

Dilly's X-ray was fine. As the doctor said, there wasn't much wrong with him at all. He got his bandage, even though he didn't really need one. And he also got the other thing he wanted . . . a ride in a wheelchair!

Mother pushed him in one from the X-ray room all the way to the dino-car.

'Mother,' said Dilly when we got home, 'about my X-ray.'

'Yes, Dilly?' said Mother. 'What about it?'

'Well, when the doctor takes a picture of what's inside my head, does that mean he can tell what I'm thinking, too?'

'No, Dilly,' Mother laughed. 'That's something *nobody* will ever be able to do!'

DILLY AND THE GHOST

'Right, Dilly,' said Father one evening at bedtime, 'what stories would you like tonight? How about *Hey Diddle Dinosaur*? It looks really good.'

'I don't want that one,' said Dilly making a face. 'It's silly. Can I have this, instead?' He reached under his pillow and handed Father a book.

'What's this?' said Father. '*The Ghost of Fern Tree Forest*? It might be a little scary, Dilly. It's one of Dorla's, isn't it?'

It was, too. Dilly is always coming into my room and taking my books. He can't read them, but he likes looking at the pictures. And ever since my Hallowe'en party, he especially wants books about witches and ghosts.

'But I *like* scary stories,' he said. 'And I want you to read it to me.'

'Well . . . ' said Father, 'I don't know, Dilly . . . '

'Please, Father,' he said. '*Please*.'

'OK, Dilly,' said Father. 'But you're to stop me the moment it gets too scary for you. I don't want you having nightmares.'

So Father started reading *The Ghost of Fern Tree Forest*. It's about a family of dinosaurs who discover their house is haunted. The doors creak and open by themselves, and something howls in the middle of the night . . .

'Well, that's quite enough of *that* for one evening,' said Father when he got to the end of the first chapter. 'I think you're a little young for this sort of thing, Dilly.'

'I'm not,' said Dilly. 'I think it's *fantastic*.' I could see he was telling the truth. Usually at story time Dilly climbs all over Father and bounces up and down on the bed. But Dilly had sat perfectly still during the story, wide-eyed and listening.

He didn't have any nightmares, either.
He made Father read *The Ghost of Fern
Tree Forest* all the way through over the
next couple of weeks. He talked about
ghosts and the story all the time.

'I liked the part where the ghost came
down the stairs,' he said one morning at
breakfast. 'Do you remember, Father? It
was really scary.'

'I certainly do, Dilly,' said Father. 'By
the way, I thought we might go to the
library later today to get some new
books for bedtime.'

Dilly smiled.

'Can I get a new ghost book, Father?'
he said. 'Please?'

'I suppose so, Dilly,' said Father with
a sigh. I could see he didn't look very
happy. Mother smiled.

'What's the matter, dear?' she said.
'I don't think your father likes ghost

stories very much, Dilly. Perhaps they're a little too scary for *him*.'

We all laughed, and I saw Mother wink at Father. I don't think Dilly did, though. He was too busy giving Father a funny look.

Dilly got a pile of ghost books from the library, and Father read him all of them. Dilly thought they were terrific.

Then one night, a very strange thing happened.

We were all sitting watching TV, when suddenly there was a creaking noise . . . *creeeeeakkkk* . . . and the sitting room door opened all by itself.

'Now that's odd,' said Father. He stood up, looked round the door into the hall, and shut it.

Mother said it was probably a draught from an open window. But none of the windows were open.

'I know what it was,' said Dilly. Everyone looked at him. 'We've got a . . . GHOST!'

'Don't be silly, Dilly,' said Father. 'There's no such thing.'

Dilly didn't say anything. But when Father wasn't looking, I could see him smiling secretly to himself. I began to realise that Dilly was up to something.

You could almost see his little mind
working . . .

At bedtime that evening, Father
started reading a new ghost story about a
haunted cave to Dilly. I could hear his
voice from my bedroom.

'And just then,' he was saying, 'there
was a noise . . . '

'Ssshh, Father,' Dilly said.

'What, Dilly?' said Father. 'What is it?'

'Ssshh . . . ' said Dilly. 'I can hear
something.'

'What can you hear?' said Father. I
thought he sounded a little . . . worried.

'I don't know,' said Dilly. 'It's a sort
of whistling, or someone going
"Whooooo " . . . '

Father went quiet for a moment.

'Oh, this is ridiculous,' he said after a
while. 'I suppose you'll be telling me
next it's a ghost.'

'It isn't *a* ghost, Father,' said Dilly.

'I'm glad to hear you say so, Dilly,' said Father.

'No . . . it's *our* ghost. The one that lives with us.'

Father got quite cross then, and said he wouldn't read any more of the ghost story if Dilly was going to misbehave. So Dilly said he was sorry, and Father kept reading.

Later, after I heard Father say good night and go downstairs, I sneaked into Dilly's room. I knew he must be up to something.

At first he wouldn't tell me. Then he said he really *did* believe we had a ghost, and he was just trying to make Father believe it too. But nothing he did seemed to work.

'It would help if Father actually saw a ghost,' I said. 'So . . . why don't *you* pretend to be one?'

I'd read a story once about someone who pretended to be a ghost. All he'd done was to put a sheet over his head and make lots of moaning noises, like the ghosts you see in TV programmes. Dilly said that was what he was planning anyway. Then he would walk down the stairs like the ghost in *The Ghost of Fern Tree Forest*.

We both thought it was a really terrific idea. Dilly jumped out of bed and pulled a sheet off right then and there. I said I'd go back to my room and wait until I heard him on the landing.

I got into bed and waited. Nothing happened for a while, although I did hear some strange noises coming from Dilly's room. I was just about to go and see what he was doing, when Dilly's bedroom door opened and the landing light clicked off.

There was a swishing noise, and a pale shape appeared in the dark at the top of the stairs. It made a really scary noise – *whoooooo* . . . , it went. *Whoooooo* . . .

Even though I knew it was only Dilly pretending to be a ghost, it made me feel shivery all over.

'Is that you, Dilly? What's happened to the light?' It was Father's voice. Dilly didn't answer. He just kept moaning and swishing down the stairs.

I peeked round my door, and just at that moment, Father turned on the light. He was right in front of Dilly, with a strange look on his face. He even seemed a little . . . scared. But when he saw what Dilly had done to his sheet, he wasn't frightened – he was very, very cross.

Dilly had cut two holes in the sheet for his eyes, and drawn all over it with his crayons. So that was what he'd been doing in his room! Father said it was completely ruined, and that Dilly was the naughtiest dinosaur there had ever

been. I said it had been my idea to use the sheet, so I got told off too.

By now, Dilly was getting upset, and when Father said he couldn't go to Dixie's the next day to play, you can guess what happened. That's right, he let rip with a 150-mile-per-hour, ultra-special super-scream, the kind that would frighten any ghost out of its wits. At least that's what Father said.

The next morning, Dilly said he was sorry.

'Well, Dilly,' said Mother, 'you were very naughty. You've ruined that sheet . . . but it *was* almost worth it to see the look on your Father's face.'

'You weren't really frightened, were you, Father?' said Dilly.

'No, of course not,' said Father.

'So will you read me a ghost story tonight?'

'Er . . . ' Father began to say. But Mother didn't give him a chance to finish.

'Of course he will, Dilly. He loves ghosts,' she said. And we all laughed – even Father!

DILLY DINOSAUR, SUPERSTAR

DILLY'S PET

'Father, can I have a pet?' asked Dilly
one day.

'What, Dilly?' said Father.

It was a lovely, sunny morning, and
we were all in the garden. Mother was
basking in the sunshine, I was reading,
Father was doing some gardening, and
Dilly was supposed to be playing. But he
was following Father around being a pest
instead.

'All my friends have got pets,' said

Dilly. 'I'm the only one who hasn't.'

Dilly had caught up with Father in the part of the garden where the swamp roses grow. They're Father's favourite flowers, and he spends ages looking after them.

Father's always telling us about the little creatures which come into the garden to eat his plants. He says there's one in particular which just loves swamp roses. It's called a Swamp Lizard, and if we ever find one in the garden, we're

supposed to tell him.

'I'm sorry, Dilly,' he said, 'but your mother and I don't think you're ready to have a pet just yet.'

'But I *am* ready, Father,' said Dilly. 'I've been ready for ages!'

'What I mean, Dilly,' said Father with a sigh, 'is that you're not old enough yet. Pets can be hard work. You have to make them somewhere to live, remember to feed them regularly and maybe even take them for walks. We think you'd probably forget to do all that.'

'But I wouldn't, Father!' said Dilly. 'I *promise* I wouldn't!'

'I'm sorry, Dilly,' said Father. 'The answer is still no. You'll just have to wait until you're older.'

'It's not fair!' shouted Dilly. 'I want a pet and I'm going to have one!' He stamped his foot, and swished his tail around, and for a second I thought he was going to have a tantrum. Father was beginning to look angry, too. Luckily, Mother came to the rescue.

'It's such a lovely day,' she said quickly. 'Why don't we all go swamp wallowing?'

Dilly soon changed his tune. He loves swamp wallowing, and he couldn't wait to go. But if Mother and Father thought he'd forgotten about having a pet, they were wrong, as we found out later . . .

The next morning, I went with Father to the Shopping Cavern to buy a new pair of shoes for school. When we got home, Mother was cooking lunch and Dilly was playing in the garden. I took the lid off the box and showed Mother my new shoes.

'They're perfect, Dorla,' she said. 'Why don't you show them to Dilly? You

can tell him his toasted fern stalks are
ready, too.'

I went into the garden, and at first
I couldn't see Dilly. Then I saw his tail
sticking out from behind the giant fern.
He seemed to be kneeling down and
looking at something on the ground.
I couldn't see what it was.

'What *are* you doing, Dilly?' I said.

Dilly jumped and looked round at me.
He stood up, but I noticed that he kept
both paws behind his back.

'Nothing,' he said. I didn't believe him, though. He had his I-Know-I'm-Doing-Something-Wrong-But-I-Don't-Care look on his face.

I told him that lunch was ready, and showed him my new shoes in the box. I thought he'd say 'Yuck!' or 'They're stupid!' like he usually does, but he didn't. In fact he didn't really look at them. He was interested in something else.

'Can I have the box?' he said. '*Please*, Dorla?'

I was so surprised he'd said 'please' that I took the shoes out and gave him the box right there and then. We went back into the house, and Dilly ran upstairs.

'Dilly!' called Mother. 'Where are you going? Your lunch is on the table!'

'Coming, Mother,' Dilly called out. He came back downstairs and sat at the table. He didn't have the shoe box with him.

Dilly was very quiet and well behaved at lunch. As you know, he usually makes a real mess with his food, and he often spills his pineapple juice. But today he didn't do any of that, although he *was* rather slow. In fact, when everyone else had finished, Dilly's plate looked as if he'd hardly started.

Father told him he'd have to hurry up and finish while the rest of us tidied our dishes away.

'I will, Father,' said Dilly. And he did, too. The moment Mother, Father and I went out of the dining room and into the kitchen, he must have speeded up a lot. For when we came back, Dilly's plate was completely empty, and he was sitting there with a big smile on his face.

'Well, Dilly,' said Father. He looked

rather surprised. 'You must have been hungry after all.'

Dilly went up to his room after that, but he didn't stay in there for very long. After a while, there was a knock on my door. I opened it, and Dilly was standing there. He gave me a big smile.

'Can I *please* borrow some of your doll's house furniture, Dorla?' he asked, very politely. 'I promise I won't break it.'

Usually I won't let Dilly near my doll's house. But he'd asked so nicely, I couldn't really say no, especially as I could see Mother standing on the stairs listening. I let him choose what he wanted, and then he went back to his room.

Mother said it was nice to see Dilly being well behaved for a change. I didn't say anything.

That's because I was sure he was up to something.

I was even more sure of it later when he did something very strange. He came downstairs with the shoe box and asked Mother if he could go into the garden. She said he could. He went outside, marched round the garden twice, came back inside, and went straight up to his room. He looked really happy.

I kept my eye on Dilly all evening, but I couldn't work out what he was doing.

The next day, Dilly asked Mother if he could go into the garden again. He had the shoe box with him, and he kept looking at it. He seemed a little worried.

'Of course you can, Dilly,' said Mother. Dilly hurried outside, and I didn't think any more about it.

A little later, Father said he was going to do some gardening. He hadn't been outside long when we heard him call out. Mother and I went into the garden. Father was standing in the part where the swamp roses grow. He looked rather upset.

'They're gone,' he said. 'Every last one of them!'

It was true. The stalks had been stripped bare. Then I noticed a petal lying on the ground, and another, and another . . . They made a trail which led us to the giant fern. We went round

behind it, and there was Dilly with his
shoe box.

'Dilly,' said Father, 'I think you'd
better show me what's in the box.'

Dilly didn't say anything. He just
stopped smiling and held on to the box
more tightly.

'Come on, Dilly,' said Father. 'Hand it
over.'

Dilly didn't hand it over. Instead, he

blasted our ears with an ultra-special, 150-mile-per-hour super-scream, the sort that sends us all diving for cover behind the nearest fern bush.

We soon discovered what it was all about once Dilly had calmed down. Inside the shoe box was a Swamp Lizard he had found and made into his pet. He'd wanted my shoe box and doll's house furniture to make it a home, and all that marching round the garden had been to give his pet a walk.

He hadn't eaten his lunch the day before, either. He'd slipped it into a pocket for his pet when we weren't looking. The lizard had drunk some pineapple juice, but hadn't touched any of the toasted fern stalks. Dilly had been worried he would starve. Then he'd remembered that there was a flower Swamp Lizards just loved to eat . . .

Of course, Father was very cross. Dilly was told off and sent to his room for the rest of the day.

Later, at bedtime, I heard Dilly say he was sorry. He also asked Father if he could keep the Swamp Lizard.

'I did all the things you said, Father. So I must be ready to have a pet.'

'I'll think about it,' said Father. Then he sighed. '*You* might be ready, Dilly – but I'm not sure if *I* am yet . . .'

DILLY — DINOSAUR SUPERSTAR

'Dilly, will you *please* stop making that horrible noise!' shouted Mother from downstairs. She sounded very cross.
'I can hardly hear myself think!'

It was even worse for me. I was in my room, which is right next to Dilly's. The noise was so bad it was beginning to make my teeth hurt and my tail twist. And he'd been doing it all afternoon.

Dilly couldn't have heard Mother, because the next thing I knew, she'd come upstairs and was banging on his bedroom door. I went out on the landing. After a while, the noise stopped and Dilly's door opened.

'What on earth are you doing, Dilly?' said Mother.

'I'm only playing a game, Mother,' he said.

'Well, can't you play it more quietly? What sort of game is it, anyway?'

'I'm playing Rex and the Rockosaurs, Mother,' said Dilly with his biggest smile. 'I'm Rex – do you like my guitar?'

I hadn't noticed before, but Dilly was holding Father's old tennis racquet just like it was a guitar. He was also wearing some funny clothes from the dressing-up box – an old, shiny top of Mother's, and a scarf all covered in spangly stars. He had a pair of toy sun-glasses on, too.

I should have realised, of course. Recently, Dilly's done nothing but talk about Rex and the Rockosaurs. I like them too, and Dilly only started being a fan of theirs to copy me. But now he thinks they're wonderful. Whenever they're on the TV, he loves to sing along with them and dance in front of the screen so that no one else can see anything.

'Very nice, Dilly,' said Mother, with a sigh. 'But why don't you stop being Rex for a while and come downstairs for a snack? You can have your favourite if you like – a swamp-worm and swamp-nut butter sandwich with a glass of pineapple juice. How does that sound?'

Dilly said it sounded terrific. But he also said he didn't want to stop being Rex, so he kept his pop star outfit on while he ate and drank.

'You know, Mother,' he said between mouthfuls, 'one day I'm going to be a superstar on TV, like Rex and the Rockosaurs.'

'I'm sure you will be, Dilly,' said Mother. 'You make enough noise for a superstar, anyway. But for now I'd like you to concentrate on being a careful little dinosaur. I'm sure Rex doesn't spill pineapple juice down *his* front.'

That evening, Rex and the Rockosaurs were on TV again. They had made a new record called *Rock Around the Swamp*, and Dilly thought it was fantastic.

'Can we get it, Mother?' he said. 'Can we? Can we?' He bounced up and down in front of her so much that his dark glasses almost fell off.

'Well, Dilly . . .' said Mother, 'I don't know about that. It's only well-behaved, *quiet* little dinosaurs who get records bought for them.'

'I promise I'll be quiet, Mother,' said Dilly. He had his I'll-Be-As-Good-As-I-Possibly-Can look on his face.

'OK, Dilly,' said Mother. 'We'll buy it at the Shopping Cavern on Saturday. Dorla, you can have a record too.'

Dilly jumped up and shouted 'Hurray!' as loudly as he could, then remembered that he was supposed to be quiet.

'Sorry, Mother,' he whispered.

'That's all right, Dilly,' Mother whispered back, with a smile.

We set out in the dino-car early on Saturday morning. It's always crowded at the Shopping Cavern, and sometimes it's difficult to find a parking space. But when we arrived, we soon realised it was more crowded than we'd ever seen it before.

We got stuck in a traffic jam, and then there didn't seem to be anywhere to park at all. We found a space at last, and went into the Shopping Cavern. It was packed. There were dinosaurs coming from everywhere, and they all seemed to be heading in one direction.

'What's going on?' said Mother.

'I don't know,' said Father. 'But if we want to get to the record shop, we'll have to follow everyone else. It's over there.'

Father pointed to where the dinosaurs were packed tightest. We joined the crowd and set off towards the record shop. It was hot, it was noisy, and everyone was pushing and shoving. Somebody even stood on my tail. After ten minutes we'd hardly got any nearer.

'This is ridiculous,' said Mother. She didn't look as if she was enjoying her trip to the Shopping Cavern one little bit. 'We'll never get there at this rate.'

Dilly looked upset. He'd gone bright green and his bottom lip had started to quiver, the way it always does when he's just about to cry.

'Does that mean I won't get my Rex and the Rockosaurs record?' he said.

Mother was just about to answer him when someone interrupted her. It was a teenage dinosaur who was in the crowd just in front of us.

'So you're a Rex and the Rockosaurs fan too,' she said to Dilly. 'I can't wait to see them . . . isn't this exciting!'

'You mean Rex and the Rockosaurs are *here*?' said Father.

'*Of course* they are,' said the teenager. 'Didn't you know? They're making a personal appearance at the record shop today to sign copies of their new single. There are TV cameras here, and everything.'

'Now we know why it's so crowded,' said Mother. She didn't look very pleased, but Dilly was absolutely delighted.

'I'm going to see Rex! I'm going to see Rex!' he kept saying. He was so happy and excited that he couldn't keep still. He pulled his dark glasses out of his coat pocket and put them on. 'Come on, Mother! *Let's go!*'

'I don't think we're going anywhere,' said Mother. 'This is impossible, Dilly. We'll have to come back another day.'

Dilly's face changed instantly.

'But I want to see Rex and the Rockosaurs, Mother,' he said.

'I'm sorry, Dilly,' said Mother, 'but I'm getting a headache, and I think we ought to go back to the dino-car.'

Dilly didn't say anything . . . he just opened his mouth and fired off an ultra-special, 150-mile-per-hour super-scream, the kind that makes a huge, noisy crowd of dinosaurs go very, very quiet all of a sudden.

Mother and Father were embarrassed, and tried to calm Dilly down, but he just wouldn't shut up. He screamed, and screamed, and screamed, and soon everyone was looking at him. After a while, a dinosaur pushed through the crowd and came up to us.

'Excuse me,' he said. Mother looked round. 'My name is Ronnie, and I'm Rex's manager. Rex was so impressed by your little dinosaur's voice that he'd like to meet him . . .'

Of course, Dilly stopped screaming *immediately*.

'Can I, Mother?' he said. 'Can I? Can I?'

At first I thought Mother wouldn't let him because he'd been so naughty. But in the end, she said it was OK. In fact, we all got to meet Rex. He came out of the record shop, and everyone started

screaming. The dino-police had to hold
back the crowd.

'Hi there,' said Rex. 'You must be the
little dinosaur with the big voice.'

Dilly just stood there with a silly grin
on his face. Then Rex asked him what he
wanted to be when he grew up, and Dilly
said he wanted to be a superstar. Rex
laughed.

'Come and see me in a few years,' he said. 'If you can sing as loud as you can scream, then I might just have a job for you in the Rockosaurs . . .'

Rex's manager gave us a signed record, and then they had to go. They got into the longest dino-car I've ever seen, and Rex waved to us as they drove off.

At bedtime that night, Dilly couldn't stop talking about what had happened. Finally he asked Mother if she thought Rex had really meant it about having a job for him. Mother said she was sure he had.

'Great!' shouted Dilly. 'I'm going to practise singing as loud as I can *every day* until then. Won't that be fun?'

Mother didn't say anything. But from the look on her face I could tell she didn't think it would be . . .

DILLY GETS JEALOUS

Now if there's one thing you can say
about Dilly, it's that he doesn't like
anyone else interfering with *his* things.

Take the other day, for instance. Dilly
was playing with a toy he got for his
birthday, a Magic Eggshell. It has lots of
different parts, and if you move them in
the right ways it turns into a dino-car, a
robot or a spaceship.

But Dilly hadn't been able to work out
how to do it yet. So when I say he was

playing with it, what I mean is that he was *trying* to play with it, but only getting more and more cross. In the end, he stood up, stamped his foot, and threw the toy down as hard as he could.

I went over and picked it up. I only wanted to help him, but I never got the chance. Dilly grabbed the Magic Eggshell and pushed me away.

'You leave that alone, smelly old Dorla!' he shouted at me. 'It's *mine*, and you're not allowed to touch it!' He opened his mouth, and for a second I thought he was going to do what he usually does when he loses his temper . . . but just then, Father came through the door.

'Now, now, you two, what's going on?' said Father.

'I was only trying to help him with his toy, Father,' I said. 'He can't do it and it's making him cross.'

'It's *mine*, and I don't want any help!' shouted Dilly. Then he stuck his tongue out at me.

Father looked up towards the ceiling.

'Sometimes, Dilly,' he said with a sigh, 'I just don't know what I'm going to do with you. You're really going to have to learn to be a little less possessive.'

'What does poss . . . pess . . . what does that word mean, Father?' said Dilly.

'It means being a horrible little dinosaur who never lets anybody touch his things, even when they just want to help or be friends,' said Father. 'If you want others to be nice to you, Dilly,

you've got to be nice to them. Now you
go up to your room and think about it
until lunch.'

Dilly came down a little later and said
he was sorry. I knew why – Father had
promised to take us to the park that
afternoon, and Dilly didn't want to miss
out on something he loves doing.

Father said he was forgiven, and we
went to the park straight after lunch.
I took my roller skates, and Dilly took
his dino-trike. But he also insisted on
bringing his Magic Eggshell along.

It was fun at the park. Dilly was on his best behaviour. We raced up and down on the track, and for once he didn't try to knock me over. After a while, we asked Father if we could go on the tree swings and the rock slide. He said we could, and also that he would look after my roller skates, and Dilly's dino-trike and Magic Eggshell.

'Hey, look!' said Dilly as we ran over to the swings. 'There's Dixie!'

Now as you probably know, Dixie is Dilly's best friend. He just loves playing with her, and I could see he was really pleased she was there. He ran over to her and started bouncing up and down the way he always does when he's excited.

'Hi, Dixie!' he said. 'What shall we play? I've got a great idea . . .'

Dixie didn't let him finish.

'I'm sorry, Dilly,' she said with a smile,

'but I can't play with you today. I'm
playing with my *new* friend, Darryl.'

Dilly hadn't noticed the other little
dinosaur who was standing just behind
Dixie. But when he did, he didn't look
very happy any more.

'But you're *my* friend, Dixie,' he said.
'And I want to play with you.'

Dixie didn't say anything. She gave Dilly a funny look, then ran off to the rock slide with Darryl.

Father went over to talk to Dixie's mother, and I had a long go on a tree swing. I was having such a good time that I didn't think about Dilly at all for a while. But when I got off the swing, I saw that he was standing by the rock slide.

Dixie was going up the steps. Darryl was about to follow her, but Dilly got in first. He pushed Darryl aside, and went up behind Dixie. I could see that he was talking to her. But she didn't say anything to him. She just went down the slide and waited for Darryl. Then they ran off together to the fern bush maze.

Dilly didn't give up, though. He followed Dixie and Darryl round the whole playground. He made lots of noise, and did all sorts of silly things to try and

make Dixie look at him. He even stood
on his head in the sandpit, and got
covered in sand from the top of his head
to the tip of his tail.

All the little dinosaurs in the
playground laughed at him and thought
he was really funny. All of them, that is
. . . except Dixie. She just wasn't
interested.

I could see that all this was making Dilly more and more cross.

Things went from bad to worse after that. Dilly still followed Dixie and Darryl around. But now he took every chance he could to get in Darryl's way. And then, by the roundabout, he even tried to trip him up.

'Dilly!' shouted Father. 'Come here at once!'

Dilly came stomping over, STOMP, STOMP, STOMP. He was looking very sulky.

'I saw that, Dilly,' said Father, 'and it wasn't very nice. If I've told you once, I've told you a thousand times – you are *not* to do that sort of thing. It can be very dangerous in a playground. You're lucky that little dinosaur was quick enough to get out of your way. And why are you being so horrible to him? He hasn't done anything to you, has he?'

Dilly didn't say anything. He just stood in front of Father with his I-Feel-Really-Mean-And-Nasty scowl on his face. Father was beginning to look quite cross.

'I think Dilly's jealous of him, Father,' I said.

'I am not!' shouted Dilly, but I took no notice.

'Dilly wants to play with Dixie, but she's playing with that little dinosaur,' I said. 'He's her new friend.'

'Well, Dilly,' said Father, 'you can't make someone play with you if they don't want to. You'll have to learn that being possessive with your friends is the quickest way to lose them.'

Father made Dilly sit on the bench next to him, and said he had to play with his Magic Eggshell. I wasn't sure if that was a good idea. He was still really sulky, and

he just couldn't make it work. It wasn't
long before he was looking even more
cross than ever.

So you can probably guess what
happened next.

That's right – Dilly threw down his
Magic Eggshell as hard as he could,
opened his mouth, and let rip with an
ultra-special, 150-mile-per-hour super-
scream, the sort that makes all the other
little dinosaurs in the playground stop

what they're doing and look at him.

Dilly calmed down at last. Father was in the middle of telling him off when Dixie and Darryl came over.

'Is Dilly all right?' asked Dixie.

'I think so, Dixie,' said Father. 'He's just being silly because he can't make his toy work.'

'Is it a Magic Eggshell? I've got one of those,' said Darryl. Before Dilly could say a word, Darryl picked up the Eggshell, and with three quick flicks, he turned it into a dino-car, then a robot, and then a spaceship. Dilly just looked at him in amazement.

'How did you do that?' he said.

'It's easy when you know how,' said Darryl. 'I'll show you if you like . . .'

Dilly sat quietly while Darryl taught him how to make the Eggshell work. After a few minutes the two of them looked as if they'd always been the best of friends. Dilly, Darryl and Dixie played together for the rest of the afternoon.

On the way home, Father said he was pleased that Dilly had learned not to be so possessive and liked Dixie's new friend.

'But he's not Dixie's friend, Father,' said Dilly. 'Darryl is *my* friend.'

Father gave Dilly a hard look. For a second I thought he was going to tell him off again. But he didn't.

He just sighed

DILLY AND THE MINDER

The other morning, the post-dinosaur brought Mother an important-looking letter. It was good news. Mother had got the job she'd applied for, and she was very pleased.

Dilly didn't really understand, so Mother had to do some explaining. She told him about how she'd given up work when I was born so she could take care of me. Father had been the one who earned the money we needed.

'Then *you* were born, Dilly,' she said, 'and I had two little dinosaurs to look after. But I always wanted to go back to work one day, and now I can. The extra money will help, too.'

I could see that Dilly was thinking very hard about all this.

'But if you go to work, Mother,' he said, 'who's going to look after . . . *me*?'

Mother gave Dilly a hug, and told him not to worry.

'We've thought about that, Dilly,' she said. 'I won't be going to work every day, and you'll be at nursery school most of the time, anyway. But when you're not, you can go to a minder. You remember what a minder is, Dilly – it's someone who looks after little dinosaurs when their parents go to work. We've already found one for you. Her name is Mrs Dolf, and she lives just around the corner.'

'But I don't want to be looked after by a stupid old minder,' said Dilly, and stamped his foot. 'I only want to be looked after by . . . YOU!'

'There's no need to shout, Dilly,' said Mother. I could see that she was trying to be patient. 'It won't be so bad. I'm sure you'll enjoy it.'

Dilly opened his mouth, and for a second I thought he was going to do what he usually does when he gets cross about something. But he didn't get the chance.

'Is that the time?' said Father suddenly, looking at his watch. 'I'd better hurry, or I'll be late for work!'

Mother said I'd be late for school, too, so we all started rushing around. All of us, that is, except Dilly, who just sat at the breakfast table with a strange look on his face . . .

That evening, Mother and Father tried

very hard to get Dilly used to the idea of going to a minder. But nothing seemed to work. They told him he wouldn't be there long, that Mrs Dolf had lots of toys for him to play with and books to read, and that she might even take him to the park sometimes – if he were a good little dinosaur.

Dilly didn't say anything. He just sulked.

'I'll take you to meet her tomorrow, Dilly,' said Mother. 'You can meet Danni, too. That's Mrs Dolf's little dinosaur . . . I think he's a bit older than you. So you'll have someone to play with. That will be nice, won't it?'

'No, it won't,' said Dilly. He stamped off upstairs to his room, STAMP, STAMP, STAMP, with his I'm-Going-To-Sulk-As-Hard-As-I-Can look on his face. Then he slammed his bedroom door behind him – SLAM!

Father told him off for being naughty, and said he had to stay in his room until bedtime.

The next morning, Mother took Dilly round to meet Mrs Dolf. When I got home from school, Dilly was upstairs in his room, and Mother was looking very cross.

The visit hadn't been a success. Dilly

had stuck his tongue out at Mrs Dolf
and called her a rude name. Then he'd
thrown a tantrum, swished his tail around
and knocked over a vase with a fern plant
in it. The vase was smashed to pieces, and
there had been a terrible mess on the rug.

Mrs Dolf had been very nice about it,
and Mother said Danni had laughed.
I guess he thought it was funny. But
Mother didn't, and when she got Dilly

home, she had told him off and sent him to his room for the rest of the day.

He came downstairs for dinner later, and said he was sorry. Mother said he would have to be much better behaved the next time they went to Mrs Dolf's, and that he would also have to save up his pocket money to pay for a new vase.

Dilly looked very thoughtful. He didn't say much more, except to ask Mother if she thought Danni had been laughing at *him*.

'He might have been, Dilly,' said Mother. 'You do look pretty silly when you're misbehaving like that.'

After that, Dilly was very quiet.

The rest of the week went quite quickly, and it wasn't long before Mother's first day at work came round.

She got up very early and spent a lot of time getting ready. She put on the new

clothes she'd bought especially for her
job. Father and I said she looked terrific.
Dilly didn't say anything.

Soon it was time for everyone to go.
Mother was going to take me to school on
her way to work. That was the easy part.

But first we had to drop Dilly off at
Mrs Dolf's.

'Come on, Dilly,' said Mother. 'Put
your coat on. We haven't got much time.'

Dilly just crossed his arms and stared very hard at her.

'I hope you're not going to be naughty, Dilly,' said Mother. 'That's the last thing I need today.' It was true. I could see she was feeling nervous enough about starting her new job without worrying about Dilly.

He still wouldn't put his coat on, though. Mother had to do it for him. He didn't help her at all. He held his arms as stiffly as he could, which made it really hard work.

'Right,' said Mother at last. She was out of breath and all green in the face. 'We're ready . . . Off we go!'

But Dilly still didn't budge. He had his I'm-Going-To-Be-As-Stubborn-As-I-Can look on his face, and that *always* means trouble.

In the end, Mother had to drag him out of the house, up the path, through the gate and along the street. Just as we were going round the corner, he grabbed hold of a fern bush and wouldn't let go.

Mother pulled and pulled, and I pulled too, and finally we managed to tear Dilly away and arrive at Mrs Dolf's front door. Mother rang the bell, the door opened, and there was a lady dinosaur with a nice face. A small dinosaur a little bigger than Dilly peeked round from behind her. That must be Danni, I thought.

'Hello, Dilly!' said Mrs Dolf. 'It's nice to see you again. Why don't you come in?'

Dilly didn't say anything. He just stood there, looking at Danni.

'I'm afraid Dilly's being a little awkward this morning, Mrs Dolf,' Mother said.

'I don't believe it,' said Mrs Dolf with a big smile. 'He'll be all right once he's come in and settled down, won't you, Dilly?'

I looked at Dilly. I was so sure he was going to scream that I had my paws over my ears already.

But he didn't. Instead, he marched straight into Mrs Dolf's house, keeping his eyes on Danni all the time. He didn't look at Mother at all, or say goodbye to her. She seemed quite upset.

'Are you sure?' she said, anxiously.

Mrs Dolf said she was. So we left, but as we walked away, I thought Mother looked as if she were going to cry.

She needn't have worried, though. When we went to pick Dilly up later, everything was fine. Mrs Dolf said he'd been a little quiet at first, so she'd had a talk with him. It turned out that he was more worried about Danni than her or being in a strange house. But Danni showed Dilly all his toys, and the two of them had soon made friends. They were playing happily together when we arrived.

In fact, Dilly was having such a wonderful time he didn't want to leave.

'Come on, Dilly,' said Mother. 'It's time to go home.'

Dilly stamped his foot, opened his mouth, and . . . that's right, you guessed it, he let rip with an ultra-special, 150-mile-per-hour super-scream, the kind that usually makes Mother cringe with embarrassment and want to hide under the nearest table.

But today she just smiled.

'For once, Dilly, I'm almost glad you don't want to do what you're told,' she said. 'I really am!'